P9-APW-057

THE FLORENTINE PAPERS

THE FLORENTINE PAPERS

THOM PALMER

PEREGRINE SMITH BOOKS

SALT LAKE CITY

First edition
93 92 91 90   5 4 3 2 1

Copyright © 1990 by Thom Palmer

All rights reserved. No part of this book may be
reproduced in any manner whatsoever without written permission
from the publisher.

This is a Peregrine Smith Book, published by
Gibbs Smith, Publisher
P.O. Box 667
Layton, Utah 84041

All the characters in this work are fictional. Any
resemblance to persons living or dead is
purely coincidental.

Design by Formaz
Manufactured in the United States of America
Library of Congress Cataloging-in-Publication Data
Palmer, Thom, 1961-
The florentine papers/Thom Palmer.
p. cm.
ISBN 0-87905-364-X
I. Title.
PS3566. A5434F57 1991
813'.54--dc20
90-49742
CIP

FOR MARY

Does one know the moral effects of food? Is there a
philosophy of nourishment?

Friedrich Nietzsche, *The Gay Science*

ONE

During the months of research and composition pursuant to the much-heralded publication of Maria Perpetua's *Spinacea oleracea*, it was I who was her tester and taster and muse. Maria said to me more than once that a muse is really just a polite euphemism for a paramour. So be it. I am the motivational and inspirational whore behind that book of spinach. There were times when I had enough iron coursing through my system to forge a battleship's hull. I nibbled enough quiche and gobbled enough eggs Florentine—embellished with Maria's rhapsodic, peerless hollandaise—that arteriosclerosis nightmares fuddled and confounded my sleep. The innumerable hours spent categorizing her countless three-by-five note cards, or allowing myself to be seduced when her experiments with purees filled her with an inexplicable prurience, caused my own work—an epic poem on Vietnam—to grind to an immutable halt.

The dedication, "To Popeye, mon ami," is not just another tongue-in-cheek element of this *jeu d'esprit*, though admittedly her work is full of arcanum and recondite asides that the nescient gourmand-belletrist would pooh-pooh as so much excelsior. Those in the know will tell you that this deference to the cartoon character is really a reference to me—a halfhearted one, I might add—not because I smoke a corncob pipe or because my forearms in any way resemble his, but because throughout the book's gestation, for five days out of seven (Maria generously desisted on weekends), I could honestly say, "I eats me spinach." Yet, despite the unstinting investment of my time, sanity, fully equipped kitchen, and circulatory system, I am not one whit better off than I was four years ago. Contrarily, my midsection is greater and my emotional state, always a tad delicate, is more friable than ever.

You must think, then, I write out of greed, but I assure you that, having waited so long to do this, the remuneration I'll now receive will be but a fraction of what I could have had, had I turned a deaf ear to my conscience and responded to the plethora of entreaties I received several years ago, when *Spinacea oleracea* was in its first immense printing. If

1

ever there was a lucrative time to compose this document, it would have been then, when Maria's book, despite its imposing title and snooty, dilettantish air, was bobbing atop the best-seller list with the irrepressible buoyancy of a beach ball. Accompanying the frenzied sale of the book were the rumors and speculation surrounding its authoress, about whom next to nothing was known. With a quirkiness that was the cornerstone of her eccentricities, Maria had decided that she would remain utterly reclusive, passionate about her privacy. Photographs for the book jacket were indeed taken; I went through the elegant and rather flattering proofs with her. But she rejected all of them and chose total self-effacement. Her reasons for this, I believe, were two-fold. The first was attributable to her fear and abhorrence of the glaring, corrupting limelight, a graceless state that she believed to be the exclusive property of the mediocre and the plebeian. The second was her shrewd sense of marketing; beneath that erudite, artistic veneer was a woman who could sell anything. She felt that, should the book's popularity begin to wane, the inaccessibility of its enigmatic authoress might prop it up a few months more.

But I chose silence, even though I was at an emotional low and particularly susceptible to the petty sirens of avarice and revenge. I patiently kept my attention on my own work, that was my only concern then and is my only concern now. You see, I am not writing this for the temporal salve of a bloated check from a major magazine, nor is this a vengeful poultice to soothe the lesions I acquired upon the dissolution of our relationship. This is merely a personal cleansing: I write now to rid myself of the nasty ghosts that still people my dreams, to flush out the obstructions that have devilishly lodged inside me. At one time a fruitful poet, my creative faculties slipped into a cruel coma somewhere between "Spinach Magnificat" and "Legumes et epinards Provençal" and have remained that way. I cannot continue in this manner. I give you, then, this unexpurgated chronicle.

TWO

I first encountered Maria Perpetua on the wharf. It was a surprisingly sultry April day, cloudless, breezy and mild, San Francisco Bay a scintillating, impeccable azure, serene and flecked with the white wedges of mainsails, the bright bursts of sun glinting off sailboats' shiny fittings. On days like this the piers and thoroughfares have a carnival atmosphere, with scads of tourists in vivid summer clothes spilling off the curbs and snarling the streets, clustering around a sidewalk performer like ants around a bit of dropped sweets, humming and laughing and squealing and crying. They stand in long, coiling lines for boat rides, for brief, expensive helicopter tours; they halt in their aimless tracks and gaze raptly at the live manikins, the rippling parabolas of Chinese kites; they point toward Alcatraz—that romantic lump of dubious note—and exchange concocted tales and erroneous lore.

Yes, I've seen a thousand such days, because I just so happen to work on the wharf, catering to these ogling mobs. If you have ever been there, then perhaps you've seen me. I am the scholarly-looking fellow in the candy-striped apron, filling Dixie cups with crab and bay shrimp and hawking them for a ridiculous fee. But I am just the vendor; my proprietor sets the prices and reaps the outrageous profits, from which I am entitled a paltry sum. I'm not complaining, however, for I could work elsewhere: I simply choose not to. The robotic repetition and overall inanity of the work is soothing to me, is a kind of paregoric to my feverish poetic exertions, and provides just enough money to pay my bills. For that is all I require: money for paper and typewriter ribbons, food and shelter, my occasional, frugal entertainments, and a remaining ducat or two to squirrel away in the event of an emergency. I am ascetic, not poor, and this asceticism provides me with a buffer against the distractions of material excess. This asceticism is the fossil fuel that keeps my creative light burning with an uncanny brilliance. At least, it was. Because on that April day, that temperate and otherwise routinely splendid day, my life began its plodding, inexorable change, its strange transmogrification, for I became lodged in the webwork of that lamia, that succubus, that enchantress of the potherb.

3

I was working hard. My disposition, usually affable, was beginning to tighten and twang just a bit from the heat, the hurly-burly glut of tourists, the dull, throbbing congestion of knotted muscles at the base of my spine. Scooping some change from the cash drawer, I felt the beginnings of a cool breeze at my back, completed the transaction, and turned to catch the refreshing air full in the face. And there she was.

She was half reclined in the jump seat of a large touring tricycle, the type propelled by those impudent, pedaling cicerones with the headphones clamped over their ears. The driver had momentarily stopped for a crowd of jaywalking sightseers, and she was so close to me that I could have reached out and touched her shoulder. She wore an airy, cream-colored dress of gauze, and the discerning sun outlined beneath it, in soft shadow, the line of her thigh, the roll of her bosom. A baize, lavender cap was cocked forward atop a silken, black, pinned-up helmet of hair, and a delicate veil of lavender tulle hung before her face. Embedded in her chubby little earlobe was a ruby-colored stone, and when she began to slowly, theatrically turn toward me, it deepened to an amaranth. Her gaze did not light on me arbitrarily, but seemed to fix on me from the moment she turned, as if she fully sensed she was being watched. Behind the veil her mouth was thick and ghostly from white lipstick, veined with tiny red cracks. Her reaction was so abstruse that it undoubtedly would have passed unseen by a person less perceptive and not as firmly fixed on her as I, for upon realizing she was being so visually caressed, she parted her lips just the tiniest bit, catching her breath in slight surprise, before relaxing in satisfied approval of the compliment. *My* look of surprise, or stupefaction, wasn't quite as subtle, yet that seemed neither to trouble nor amuse her. We were like two creatures who have always seen each other through the unbreachable barrier of a fence or cage and then, by some adventitious twist, are face to face, autonomous and unfettered, and therefore thoroughly unable to grasp the unthinkable situation in which they find themselves.

And yet she was beyond that fundamental level: a demiurge, an oracle, aloof and bemused, gazing steadily at me from the hallowed jump seat, displaying none of the self-conscious fidgeting that tends to overcome those who suddenly realize they are being gawked at by a stranger.

Do not ask me what was going through my head during this encounter; it is impossible for me to say. The Passage of Time is one of man's theoretical constructions, and the very fact that it only exists because we are there to perceive it makes it imperfect. It is merely our consciousness traipsing about an unmetered cosmos, and just because we assign this traipsing to ticks of the clock does not mean that time is actually passing when we become inextricably lodged in those pristine moments that invariably occur in each of our lives. Since time is a human conception, it is not the flawless, unpitted plane that we make it out to be but is instead full of lacunae into which we will inevitably plummet. While in these cavities, time is not Time, but a dense region that I can only think to call the Absolute Moment, where our preconceived notions of reality no longer apply. The minutiae gleaned and the sensations they foster all have their own space, and yet come together in this Absolute Moment in an utterly inconceivable way. The Absolute Moment has the rare quality of not existing at all and simultaneously being of such duration that one feels, were he being casually observed by a third party, he might be mistaken for someone dead on his feet. But, in this realm of "Reality" that we unquestioningly embrace, I had simply leveled a uniform, curious glance of two or three "seconds."

Time is nil and the World is a vague and not-very-cogent idea. The circumstances of the Absolute Moment fold themselves around us like petals, and the instance is retained in our memory in the same manner. While other recollections may fade or flower with age and distance, the Absolute Moments are eloquent holes of verisimilitude back into which we can crawl at any time. Be they comic or tragic or blissful or obscene, they will always retain their true form, and are impervious to any psychological voodoo we may employ in the hopes of altering them. Some are soothing, quaint regions that warm us, provide us with succor. Others are inhospitable, hyperborean places that we wish we could fill and permanently seal, that have done nothing but create slubs in the weave of our existence. The only thing that does change is the gravity we give such moments. And this one in particular, to an extent which I have not yet fully related, was for the longest time of the first, demulcent order.

The Moment propels us oftentimes to do things that we do not understand. When describing the episode, beneficiaries or victims of an Absolute Moment often say, "I don't know what made me do this, but . . ." And so it was, under the impetus provided by this strange state, that I reached behind me, and made an offering of a cup of crab and a slice of sourdough to this woman in the jump seat. Her smile widened the slightest fraction as she took my gift, and at that juncture a boat whistle mournfully droned, the jaywalkers moved off, the breeze abated, and the cicerone—with a burst of pumping legs—jerked the tricycle away. I was lifted from the pit and plopped back down into the physical world, with my legs trembling and a slight basting of sweat along my brow.

When I am in the midst of a long poem, making admirable—though slow—progress, I seldom loiter after work, or even concern myself with taking nourishment right away, but instead proceed directly home and sit right down to compose. These heated moments, when I make an unwavering and almost desperate beeline for my desk, usually see me produce my most trenchant verse. It is only after perhaps two or three hours, when my brain begins to go slightly limp and I can no longer ignore my stomach's rapacious growling, that I fix myself something to eat and then relax with a book, a jigger of Irish whiskey, or sometimes—if I've given in to a desire to splurge (after an episode of composition that was more prolific than I could ever have imagined)—a chillum of hashish. Or, if so inclined in my earlier, happierdays, I paid a call to a certain preferred house of mine, and reveled in the articulate and elegant favors of a woman known simply as Yvette.

This lovely girl, with shoulders as white and velvety smooth as bechamel, and adolescent, nose cone breasts, had, of all things, a withered left foot, an unfortunate defect of birth that had been too long ignored to be properly corrected. Though I pitied her being encumbered with such a defect, it was nevertheless irrevocable, and over the course of our engagements it developed for me a certain innocent charm, as well as an intoxicating seductiveness. To see Yvette haltingly, intrepidly move toward me across her tiny quarters, the yellowish lamplight gleaming off the coils and curlicues of her ashen hair, filled me with a generous passion that constricted my throat and quickened my pulse.* More than once I had offered to rescue her, to take her away from that place, to keep her and educate her, to save her any further indignities and even—if our rendezvous had been a particularly heady and heartrending one—to marry her. And though one would think that she would leap (figuratively) at such an opportunity, having admitted—in snippets of postcoital conversation—that she bemoaned her lot in life, she always tearfully, gratefully declined, feeling that she was tethered to that house, convinced that some humans are just bound to their predicaments, and that my affinity for her would dissipate once she had attained manumission. Besides, she assuaged her unhappiness over her station with ravaging bouts of dipsomania and assured me that the last thing I needed on my hands was a drunken mistress. Though my pleas were sincere and not just contrite bursts of altruism, I always came away slightly relieved my offer hadn't been accepted, feeling that she was perhaps correct.

But we're losing the thread. As I said, such were my habits on productive days. On this queer day, however, I was in a period of creative stasis, having just finished one canto on my Indo-Chinese epic and uncertain about how the next would begin. And when my poetic vision was not so keen, I spared myself the agony of contemplating a blank, unfriendly page and meandered about the city, stopping for a sandwich, a beer, browsing through bookstores. These unstructured moments sometimes yielded bits of verse or scraps of ideas which, if appealing enough, roosted in my head until I could get somewhere to write them down.

* You are the procuress of the poet's pain / the voice that intones his plighted troth, / that clarifies his insipid bane, / and reduces it to a sweetened broth. . . ("Ode to Amuse," 1979)

Occasionally they pertained to the work at hand, and other times were just the ingredients of an observation that might figure in a future work. That day my encounter with the woman in the jump seat was particularly nagging, the kind of isolated event that is often the basis for a good short poem, a tiny, meditative, satisfying piece.

Nestled amidst the curio shops, souvenir booths, and overpriced restaurants of Pier 39 is a decrepit and thoroughly unpretentious bar (the name of which I must withhold) patronized by the working-class members of the wharf and other local denizens. This sleepy place has remained unsullied by the burgeoning influx of tourists and their indiscriminate spending. Its scuffed and patinated Wurlitzer plays at a modest volume, so that one may carry on a normal conversation. Behind the old oak bar is one amiable woman who takes her time and will remember you after your second visit. Pinned to the wall are faded black-and-white snapshots from decades gone by of waxen-faced men in fedoras or dungarees, crate hooks dangling from their belts like giant apostrophes. The wood-planked walls, scarred and rickety tables, and low-wattage lights give the interior the look of a living daguerreotype, friendly and tranquil. From its tiny, weather-beaten balcony one can survey a large portion of the wharf, the comings and goings on the esplanade.

There are many vistas in and around this beautiful chunk of coast, but the one from the balcony of this café was, and is, my personal favorite. And it was there I sat at impending dusk, looking out silently over the cityscape, at the sun-brilliant towers of the Golden Gate, the silhouetted superstructure that supports the stupendous letters spelling out Ghirardelli. Roller-skating girls in striped shorts, their hair unfurling behind them, wove through the crowds; children eating ice cream and kicking their burned legs sat along the walls of immense ovate wells brimming with red geraniums, with rhododendrons, with bluebonnets. The bobbing tour boats were disgorging their last group of passengers for the day. On the pavement directly below me, strollers slowly parted and moved aside as an empty phaeton clopped by, tringing its bell, its young, frock-coated driver tipping his stovepipe hat. I smiled, content, content with all of it, and sipped my beer. It was then I realized, from a tendril of smoke that stretched out before my face, from a slight movement peripherally registered, that someone stood next to me.

It is astonishing to me how a number of incredibly ordinary instances that occur perhaps a thousand times a day can, out of a billion or so possible combinations, come together in such a way as to produce one extraordinary circumstance. A group of people deciding to jaywalk by my place of work just as that particular cyclist was coming by, a breeze wafting in off the bay at the exact moment I had finished a transaction and decided to turn around, and then my subsequent impulsive decision to stop that evening at that café—much like the explosion that formed our solar system and capriciously deposited this spinning sphere in the one and only location possible for the evolution and support of the highest forms of life we know—fatefully linked me with this woman. (I recall one amazing sequence from the not-too-distant past. Sitting down to compose a letter to an acquaintance, I glanced at my watch for the date and noticed that it was 12:34, 5/6/78. This troubled me slightly, scattered my thoughts, and I was unable to write very much and therefore put the letter away, deciding to continue after I'd gotten some sleep. Forgetting that numerical oddity after a refreshing snooze, I took up my pen and was on the verge of picking up where I had left off when something caused me to glance at my watch again, and I saw that it was 12:34 P.M. on the very same day. I was so thoroughly spooked that I destroyed the letter for fear that this double occurrence was some sinister sign that did not bode well for my correspondent should I complete and mail that missive, as if while reading it he might inadvertently stick his finger in a light socket or absentmindedly saunter into the path of an oncoming beer truck. It seems preposterous, but these things happen.)

I remember thinking something peculiar might occur. She drew on her cigarette and smiled at me. Her full, engaging lips, glossy from their fresh coating of white and flecked with a sliver or two of tobacco, looked like nougat. Before me on the railing, she set her empty Dixie cup.

"How about a taste of that beer?" she said, and dropped her lit butt over the side of the balcony. I expected someone's scream from below, but none came. Tilting her cup, I poured her a slow, swirling, headless beer. A few shreds of crab bobbed about in the amber effervescence.

THREE

S he was born Maria Pengguling in a squalid apartment in the Tenderloin, on the very same salvaged, wafer-thin mattress, she assured me, upon which she had been conceived. Due to the gypsylike, communal nature of her parents' existence, there was, and is, no formal record of the birth and only one other witness besides her mother, an ex-prostitute named Mrs. al-Habim. Maria fixes the date as April 24 and is relatively certain that the year was 1960, since, as the story goes, her mother was participating with her communal cohorts in a round-the-clock celebration of Shakespeare's birthday, which consisted of (among other, no doubt, unmentionable activities) the rendering of the bard's plays with frenzied, decadent, bacchanalian spoofs of Elizabethan court dancing by cast and audience between acts. It goes without saying that this orgiastic marathon was a bit much for the incredibly pregnant woman. So fervent and heartrending was her portrayal of Ophelia that, during her mad scene, she induced labor. Whipped into a froth by her regular, intermittent pain, she brought the attendant coterie to near delirium with what they considered to be the most poignant piece of method acting they had ever seen. Mrs. al-Habim, no longer able to stand the katzenjammer thundering above her, stormed the apartment and found the poor Miss Pengguling moaning in the wings of the makeshift stage, being calmed by Polonius, who did not realize that the woman was on the verge of having a child, but simply thought that she had delved too deeply into her part. Somehow Mrs. al-Habim, in her broken and intimidating English, got the revelers to vacate the apartment (they moved their festival to someone else's digs down the hall) and attended to Maria's mother through her long and arduous labor. (I gathered this information from a former member of that avant-garde lot I managed to track down, now a respectable employee of a brokerage firm, under the assurance that he would remain unidentified. His begrudging recollections were invaluable in the reconstruction of Maria's early environment. Though he was agitated that someone had dug up his lamentable, youthful affiliation with that depraved troupe, a moist, melancholy look came over him as he recalled his portrayal of Laertes and his fine handling in his climactic scene of the rapier that was, he admitted, an antenna he had torn from a hapless Plymouth parked down the street.)

11

No one can pinpoint the time of her birth, though Maria once said that she was an actress from the very start, her first cacophonous cries mingling with the troupe's caterwauling as they enacted the initial squall in *The Tempest*. My source, though addlepated and punchy by that time, believed this performance to be around the thirty-seventh or thirty-eighth hour of the celebration, which would put Maria's entrance into the world somewhere between 1:00 and 2:00 P.M. With such auspicious beginnings, a person's subsequent impact on the world would not appear so fortuitous or extraordinary.

Maria's biological father, Rolly Hills (most certainly a nom de plume), was an itinerant and negligible poet with (I am paraphrasing Laertes here) morbid affectations, until he fell under the unsavory influence of Burroughs, Michaux and peyotl (and a state of consciousness that won him unanimously the title role in Shakespeare's birthday production of *Hamlet*). Given to absences of varying duration, he disappeared shortly after Maria's arrival and it is generally accepted that he ended up as a John Doe in the city morgue, most likely oblivious to the fact that he had become a father.

Cubby Pengguling was a docile, epicene young woman with close-cut, pixieish hair, high, sharp, aristocratic cheekbones, and a tiny retroussé nose. She was an artist. Though her work esthetically is relatively unremarkable, her output was voluminous, as if the plateau to which she aspired, unattainable through the quality of her paintings, might be reached by sheer, tireless quantity. This is not to say that she was entirely devoid of talent. The paintings done during her second and third trimesters, and after Maria's arrival, are particularly joyous, vibrant, and colorful. It seems that some of her onerous predilections had fallen away, allowing her more unprincipled *faux-naif* emotions—red and green and yellow emotions of delightful lightness—to rise to the surface in celebration, to manifest themselves as veritable epiphanies engendered by motherhood. It was as if childbearing had helped open her eyes wider than ever before and flooded them with the ineffable intensity of nature and the world. No doubt Rolly Hills's retreat into the narcotic netherworld, and eventually the real netherworld, aided the unleashing of these feelings in Cubby, whose prior work had degenerated into drab, dreadful earthtone chiaroscuros that would hardly have been worth exhibiting in tandem with Hills's gloomy, threadbare verse.

So Maria's very arrival occasioned the evolution of her mother's work. But, by the same token, it also assisted in the cessation of Cubby's development. Cubby's work was primarily landscapes, vistas and still lifes and after a time, her vision and imagination had been stretched to the limit by this subject matter; her paintings were becoming repetitive and insipid. Having no formal training, she could not get a grasp on where her work should go. She was unskilled with human forms and thus intimidated by them, though one must give her credit for trying. Her works that incorporated individuals, therefore, lacked detail, and were self-conscious and consequently uninspired. Also she could no longer live the bohemian, hand-to-mouth existence of the poor artist, since a child's health was at stake. She abandoned her communal cohorts to spare Maria the unbridled debauchery, took another apartment in the building, and secured a waitressing job to pay for food and shelter. These new responsibilities forced her to relegate painting to her remaining meager hours.

She painted in the early morning, or late at night, when the light was not as supple, when the city was still swaddled in the crisp and somber fog. And then, as if crushed beneath the constraints of time and responsibility, as if her soul had suddenly jettisoned every last vestige of patience and diligence, she became consumed with an almost-hypnotic infatuation for the Jackson Pollock school of drip-and-dribble painting. Her canvases from that time are all but indistinguishable from one another, thoroughly devoid of even the tiniest morsel of that panache, that *joie de vivre* that had at one time flourished in her landscapes; they were the work of a spent, exhausted sycophant. The amount of oils wasted on such lackluster, unsatisfying work, and the prohibitive cost of restocking them, caused Cubby Pengguling to fold up her easel for good.

But this did not happen before Maria had had the opportunity to reap the benefits of an early artistic environment. Her formative years were infused with color and creativity. Her memory stretched back as far as three or four, to a world surfeit with enamels and acrylics with which she was encouraged (under supervision) to experiment. Their tiny apartment, she recalled, was dazzling and brilliant, brimming with aquarelles tacked to walls and doors, with resplendent renderings of parks a rich and fertile green, of meadows as yellow as lemons and canaries, of bodies of water a fierce and invigorating azure. Mother and daughter wallowed in whorls and swatches of lavender and topaz, raspberry, cobalt and emerald. Maria's fingers, before they were dexterous enough to manipulate a brush, were their own implements, recreating in pudgy outline the trees and buildings, the onions and apples and various vessels of still lifes. By the time she could handle a brush, her perceptions were keen enough to recognize certain nuances of texture and light.

One of these early precocious works—with an astoundingly legible signature in the lower right-hand corner: "Maria P., Age 5"—is a gouache depicting a wire basket filled with brown eggs. Her comprehension of their ovoid symmetry, of the subtle depth in their arrangement, and her heroic efforts at capturing the elusive distinctions of shade and varying gradations of brown all merge in a work that bombinates with the impalpable elements of raw genius. Though Maria dismisses it as childish folderol, I have no doubt that with a little learned direction, she could have been producing work worthy of exhibition in just a handful of years.

And when she wasn't frolicking through the garden of their Tenderloin atelier, she was in the company of Mrs. al-Habim, who sat with Maria while her mother worked. It was there without question that the buds of culinary enlightenment and experimentation began to open, for she was not repulsed by the alien aromas or foreign appearances of different dishes prepared for her and Mrs. al-Habim's lunches, but ravenously inquisitive. As in painting, where she was discovering that seemingly disparate and bold primary colors would, with certain commingling, blend into calm and copacetic shades, so it was in cooking, where ordinary—and sometimes, to her tender tongue—unpalatable foods and spices could be combined to exquisite conclusions. She testifies to this awakening in the introduction to *Spinacea oleracea:*

> I was burdened at a terribly early and impotent age with the awareness that lunches and brunches were not plates and bowls filled with piping hot substances known simply

as "food," but were the products of an assured and expert brand of alchemy—complete with beakers and retorts and burners—the fruits of a vastly innovative and creative research that had existed from time immemorial, a research that could reach heights of immense complexity and utter simplicity, could be at one moment baroque, and another austere. Cooking was a branch of knowledge that combined the highest aspects of both science and art, was virtually inexhaustible: an edifying world without end. And behind its multifarious concoctions—like musical scores or lyric poems in the public domain, accessible and accepted when one altered or embellished them and called them their own—were these magical scraps, these rapturous formulas known as recipes . . .

(I cannot read that excerpt without Strauss's *Also Sprach Zarathustra* resounding in my head, the bombastic timpani parts pounding my skull.)

While I am not shortchanging the young Maria's intellectual capacities, the above passage surely encompasses a skein of realization spread out over a much longer period of time than just the couple of cognizant years she spent in the unintentional tutelage of Mrs. al-Habim. And, by her own admission, her baby-sitter did not possess the spectrum-spanning range of diversification of which Maria so sweetly sings in the above excerpt. She did, however, offer an alternative to the type of fare Maria refers to as "The Black-and-White School of Cooking, of food prepared with pepper and served with salt; where the plate is yin and yang: one side dark and meaty, the other side light and starchy. Or, if the meat should happen to be light—fish or poultry breasts—then the starch portion is very often darkened, perhaps by frying, or camouflaged beneath some opaque, gelatinous sauce." At Mrs. al-Habim's her taste buds were quite literally assaulted with saffron and cinnamon, with hummus that was (in her amygdaloid hindsight) a bit too tart, with vegetables that were not the vapid and cooked-to-mush obligatory third party of the meal, but preferred guests, roasted to a firm and pithy texture, plangent with curry. It was there she learned that onions were not pungent and odious things that were best left on canvas, but possessed a toothsome sweetness that took just the slightest effort to coax forth. Maria would sit on the apartment floor and flip through the pages of splashed and oil-stained cookbooks, lingering over the occasional glossy, airbrushed photographs of completed recipes, the room redolent with lamb. She must have absorbed the muskiness of that particular meat, for the moistness beneath her arms exuded the same heady smell, I found, when her perspiration would glaze my fingertips.

But this blissful and evocative period of discovery was short-lived. Although Maria read, wrote, told time, and exhibited an aptitude for a degree of abstract thought that was still some years down the road for her coevals, she had never been near a classroom, while other children her age had already entered second grade. Whether or not Cubby felt she could oversee her daughter's formal education was immaterial: she did not believe her child could progress normally if she was bereft of socialization with her age group. No matter how much she learned, languishing in the squalid apartment in the heart of the unsavory Tenderloin was not the proper environment for a young girl. So Cubby—her paints depleted, her easel sold—discontinued the estrangement that had existed between her and her own parents, and she and Maria trundled off by Greyhound to Cubby's western Pennsylvania hometown.

The information on the following period of her life is scant. What I relate is paraphrased Maria: she was disinclined to talk about this time, but did let fly with dollops of detail under considerable duress from yours truly (and these were often peppered with scatological references that, in the interest of taste, I have deleted). And her grandmother finally responded to my countless inquiries with a brief note requesting I stop writing to her, "as I don't know of what you're talking about. I don't have any such granddaughter."

The next dozen-or-so years of Maria's life were an inexorable period of desuetude. Her grandparents' home was located in a sooty and sulphurous steel town, where the world did not seem quite bright enough, the water not quite clean enough, and where life seemed to exist at all only through considerable determination and perseverance. From her bedroom—an unexpected nook of privacy that made things only a trifle more bearable—she could see the turgid, pewter Ohio River, an unexciting waterway that never held a pleasure craft, only dirty,

16

sluggish tugs and plain, cumbersome barges heaped black with coal. The summers were oppressive and humid and "made every exposed surface an adhesive." The winters brought a cold that burrowed all the way into one's penetralia. Even the first big snowstorm she had ever seen was only a disappointingly brief reprieve, for it was not the purifying coating she had envisioned it to be, but instead another grey and uninviting aspect, another impediment to nature.

In relation to the grim outdoors, the interior of her existence was an anomaly. Coddled and cloistered, her grandparents devised a world of girlish fluff and pink, puffy nonsense, showering her with dubious keepsakes, with toys and trinkets that served no other purpose beyond being displayed on her dresser or propped up in a tiny rocking chair, where they would look "pretty" or—to Maria's chagrin—"cute" (the diamond hardness of that single-syllable word became Maria's fingernails-down-the-blackboard and never failed to cut her to the quick.) Snapshots from those times, invariably from their Christmases (as if no other occasion warranted the taking of photographs), show a dark-haired, doe-eyed girl in some frilly garment, her face stoic with Beethovian intensity, a monstrous stuffed beastie smiling stupidly at her side. Other shots, preceded by insufferable pleas for cheese saying, froze her face in sneers so full of disdain that I am amazed the person behind the camera did not turn to stone.

She described one Christmas that had particularly galled her. In anticipation of the upcoming yule, Grandmother Pengguling would spend long days in her kitchen baking (Maria stressed the looseness of that verb) emasculated gingerbread men, tree-shaped sugar cookies, fruitcakes (light on the fruit), wine cookies (heavy on the wine), and shortbread *ad nauseam*. Maria was, of course, permitted to watch but, despite the weighty hints she kept dropping, was refused access to the tools and ingredients so that she might try her own hand. (This is unconscionable: imagine what the world would be like if Mozart—a pianistic and harpsichordian prodigy at a tender seven—had been denied the use of said instruments; if Picasso's father, a meager artist, had told his son, "Look but don't touch. Go play with your blocks!") Instead, as a tonic to keep her happy and distracted, her grandparents presented her on

17

Christmas morning a toy oven (all the rage that year), where the budding baker could, under strict instruction, with absolutely no room for improvisation, produce treacly little hockey pucks that were supposed to be frosted and consumed, to the detriment of dignity and tooth enamel. In a scene I would sacrifice an appendage to have witnessed, the precocious Maria, aghast and momentarily speechless—a state her grandparents probably misconstrued as paralyzed glee—leveled a protracted look at the nettlesome device, and then pounced on it so ferociously that, in the few seconds before they could pull her away, she inflicted irreparable damage on the toy, vehemently declaring that she despised Christmas and intended to adopt the Judaism of her semitolerable schoolmate Brenda. (In her less suffocating household, Brenda was already responsible for preparing the family's kreplach—"Wonderful, savory stuff," Maria recalled with a slippery smile that seemed almost prurient.)

Maria's behavior became increasingly confounding. Her indifference to Catholicism, which was metamorphosing into a blatant disregard, was terribly problematic for her grandmother. This rejection of pomp and dogma was not solely attributable to the isolated Christmas traumas, but arose from the choking atmosphere of religiosity—like a billowing censer being swung beneath her nose—that pervaded the entire Pengguling household. When she wasn't being watched by catatonic teddies and dolls with polyurethane faces, she was under the ethereal gaze of some imposing, nimbus-headed Jesus picture, some agonizing crucifix, some woodcut of the Last Supper, some statuette of the Virgin. Just inside the front door on the entranceway wall was a plastic glow-in-the-dark font of holy water that Grandma Pengguling kept faithfully replenished, and which Maria was obliged to dip into and bless herself with at the outset of each and every excursion. Maria was becoming aware that her life that had begun as discovery and intellectual exploration had turned into one of indoctrination. This is not to say that she was perverse or rebellious by nature. Thoughts and ideas were, however, being forced on her without explanation, without logical reason, like the adherence to some outmoded filial traditions or—more in keeping with her view of things—some genetic disorder passed down from one generation of Penggulings to another without question or hope of cure. She dutifully acquiesced, in response to her mother's intermittent intimations "not to rock the boat," to her First Communion, her confirmation, her catechism, her domestic restrictions, but without a clear understanding of why she was doing what she was doing. Everything appeared hollow and meaningless; she began considering herself a nonentity, as fuzzy and worthless as the puerile animals that cluttered her room, her brain and personality like the stiff, unnatural joints of those dolls that existed only for someone to twist and bend their posture into fetching and alluring poses.

In all fairness her grandparents weren't tyrants or religious zealots. They were simply elderly, benevolent sorts who had suddenly been thrust into the role of parenting a young girl. If blame is to be fixed, Cubby Pengguling must bear the brunt, for it seems that at the first opportunity to resign from responsible motherhood, she leapt wholeheartedly, and assumed the position of a far older, distracted, disinterested sister to Maria, popping up now and then with entreaties that Maria not disobey her "Grandma and Grandpa, who were doing so much to make her happy." But grandparents, for lack of anything better to do, can be doting and cloying, overbearing as well as overindulgent, and it takes—in most cases—the contemporary sensibility of a parent to, either openly or secretly, ally herself with the child and tip the scale back in the other direction so evenness may be maintained. Cubby unfortunately was a miserable ally. Upon returning to Pennsylvania, she had quickly secured a job with a travel agency through an old friend. When she wasn't working, dating, dining out, or pursuing the appurtenances of a middle-brow existence, she was taking off on short junkets and package-deal cruises that she had assisted in arranging. She was rarely around long enough to witness the tempestuous wrath of Maria's festering discontent, which was beginning to manifest itself in outbursts of vulgarity and blasphemy, in the raging dismemberment of toy bears and monkeys.

So when the fur (and stuffing) went flying, it was Maria's grandparents who were usually the pitiable focus. And when they pleaded with Cubby to take her daughter in hand, they were met with Cubby's patented "As soon as I get back" (a response that became so ignominious that, whenever Maria or her grandmother were railing at one another in the heat of some trivial dispute where their tempers were frighteningly wroth, someone always spat out that scornful reply).

The shortcomings of her eastern life were manifold. Maria was gifted: her mother knew this, her teachers suspected it, and yet none of the involved parties seemed to know what to do about it. She was never placed in any accelerated programs, never given the kind of cerebral nurturing that is absolutely indispensable to prevent the atrophy of an agile mind. Her esurient intellect was not being properly fed, and her education was so unsatisfyingly inane that it ultimately achieved a kind of critical absurdity, and became a lot of trumpery that ceased to warrant her acknowledgment, let alone her attention. What followed, then, was a period of habitual truancy, with Maria taking refuge in an unseen corner of the local library. In one thirty-day stretch she read all of Proust, with intermittent forays into the food sections and restaurant reviews of myriad periodicals. She scoured Faulkner, Poe, Dostoevsky, Melville, Shakespeare, Tolstoy, Montaigne, Voltaire, Hume, Brillat-Savarin, Schopenhauer, fairy stories, folktales, gathering names, and canvassing anthologies, histories, geographies, "anything that seemed like it was something I should read."

By day she was sated with literature, a cornucopia of Great Ideas. As rich and turbulent as her mind became, however, the dusty hours spent amidst stacks of aging books were not sufficient to ward off ennui. To give her life a more robust flavor, she started spending her evenings consorting with what is commonly described as "the wrong sort." She kept company with one fellow in particular, identified only as Joe, whom she characterized as a "rudimentary Machiavellian." This Joe, when not preoccupied with the care, feeding, and acceleration capabilities of his rebuilt Barracuda, concerned himself with reducing Maria to various states of undress. She did not, she asserts, harbor any romantic delusions, was fully aware of the narrow objective of marauding hormones, and kept their relationship "functional" by maintaining a levee of piety and virtue. Though it was not her original intention, she did, in fact, use him, and Joe would no doubt find that rather hard to believe, simply because she used him so deftly. He was her first, unwitting muse. Crass and illiterate, Joe provided a seamy and daring underside to her milieu. She discovered that the probing of his scarred and ruddy hands, the greedy urgency of his acrid, tobaccoey kisses, helped the ideas massed inside her brain to gush forth, and it was during their affiliation that she began her first work: a play, of all things, called *The Intarsia of Flavors.*

The work is abysmal, a pastiche of Shavian parlor patter and Shakespearean tragedy. The play concerns a fashionable, celebrated gourmet and culinary columnist for an influential eastern newspaper, a Mrs. Driscoll, and her society friends. Among these friends is a young man named Modrian Torpor, son of famed restauranteur Abraxis Torpor, whose Asymptote Inn always garners a "Five Exclamation Point" rating in Mrs. Driscoll's annual "Eatery Analysis," not necessarily for the quality of its cuisine but because of the hefty, illicit monetary gifts the elder Torpor bestows on the columnist. Unbeknownst to the coterie, as well as Abraxis, the impetuous Modrian, "his eyes a keen, piercing Mediterranean blue, his Greco-Roman features lovely to the point of distraction," writes a column for a rival publication under the pseudonym "The Palate." His unique approach to the kitchen and to food writing is often the subject of disparaging conversation at Mrs. Driscoll's soirees, where he is referred to as "The Cleft Palate," and his remarks and observations are trodden upon by the elite crowd as "radicalism's new extension" and "the Marxist approach to dining out." The Palate's true identity is known at the outset only by Kiki, Mrs. Driscoll's daughter, who is carrying on a torrid, secret affair with Modrian, and who is madly jealous of the fawning looks given him by a goodly number of the older, married ladies who attend these gatherings. Though the entire first act of *Intarsia* takes place in Mrs. Driscoll's dining room, all this information is revealed to us through horrendously contrived asides and brief snatches of time alone between principal characters. Though I do not have a copy of the play (there is only one and Maria, of course, has taken it with her, if not destroyed it), I took the liberty of committing some scenes to memory should an occasion such as this ever arise:

[The guests mill about the table. A sharp bang is heard offstage.]

MRS. DRISCOLL: My goodness, what was that?

MR. BOGGLE: I say, it sounded like a shot, or a backfire perhaps!

21

MRS. DRISCOLL: Maybe Charles has fallen down the stairs again. Someone please come with me.

[All exit except for Modrian and Kiki. They embrace.]

KIKI: O Modrian, I can't stand those old bags gawking at you!

MODRIAN: Surely you don't think I find it comforting, my pet?

KIKI: I don't know what you think anymore, Modrian. Our rendezvous are so brief, thanks to your paper and its damn deadlines. I wish you would stop writing that despicable column. If mother ever found out who you were, we'd never see each other again. I can't bear the thought. I'd rather die.

MODRIAN: You just might. I thought the cutlets were indecently underdone. Shh, the guests are returning!

And so on.

The remainder of the first act plods through dinner. By the time the second act rolls around, our tyro has tired of, or cannot sustain, the not-so-witty repartee, and the plot turns ugly. Modrian is found brutally murdered, his tongue cut out, his mouth stuffed with his own newspaper clippings. Kiki, gorged on nepenthean sedatives, tells all she knows. High society is all agog, fingers get pointed, damning evidence turns up in Mrs. Driscoll's bed, and so many odd elements are folded into the whole batter that the play expires of its own weight, and Maria mercifully allowed it to rest in peace.

The play's death coincided with the progression of her physical relationship with Joe. The pettings and pawings carried out in the back seat of the Barracuda had reached their pinnacle. Maria had hoped to prolong their mutual carnal curiosity throughout the development of her material, but the act of writing took far longer than she had imagined it would, and the momentum of lust was such that to divert it from its natural destination any further might have caused a backlash, an irrevocable rift. Maria was in a quandary, too deeply immured in both activities to forsake either one, yet she should have realized (and she eventually did) that it is far easier to find another lover in this world than it is to revive and revamp a dead piece of writing. In my estimation there still flickered a flame or two of creative naiveté in this nubile young woman: Joe was her first muse, and perhaps she was reacting to a feeling of blind obligation. But this is all elementary. Whatever thoughts were clashing in her moiling sensibilities, the couple's fructifying passion was consummated, and *The Intarsia of Flavors* was aborted.

Each failure preens us for success. Maria rather quickly quit her relationship with Joe: their couplings had become for her tiresome rote and had ceased to be grist for her mill. A new idea took shape, a new plan was conceived, and to see it through, she had to "reform" somewhat. Her absenteeism fell off to keep up appearances, and with the influence of one of her mother's male admirers—a golf pro at a local country club—she got a job waitressing in the lounge of that establishment. It was not difficult for this girl, with an intelligence beyond her years and a disarming, esoteric smile that she employed with surgical precision, to become the favorite of some of the most hardened, haughty club members, and therefore the beneficiary of their most generous gratuities. (This is not all as smooth as it sounds, for Maria's success with the patrons did not go unnoticed by the other waitresses. Their looks were always on her, trying to discern the sickeningly obsequious behavior they were certain existed, some servile manner that made her the darling. Instead what they saw was a girl far less bubbly and effusive than any of them, with a controlled, methodical politeness, who showed utter equanimity to customers and co-workers. Since she was devoid of any overt kowtowing and bootlicking, her popularity was an even more complex puzzle, and since they could not localize their hate in any one aspect of her, they despised her all together. Intending to rankle and perturb her they sometimes pulled pranks, like stealing her food orders when the kitchen sent them up, or taking the check she would present to her customers and scrawling on the reverse phrases such as "I'm not wearing underpants," or "Eat dog!" What these imps did not know, however, was that Maria's sangfroid was an act, and one trait she had developed, when she'd finely tuned a role, was never to step out of character. She was unflappable, and with this composure could explain any indiscretion or inconvenience her co-workers perpetrated in such a way that she ofttimes received larger tips than she would have if nothing had been amiss.)

She squirreled her earnings away, stashing an ever-increasing wad of bills in the battery chamber of an old doll. She took meticulous care to avoid any frays with her grandmother, acquiescing to most demands put on her (which steadily decreased in inverse proportion to her new course of cooperation), and even resumed attending mass (a tack she was wary of trying, for fear she might arouse suspicion of her ulterior motives.) But her grandparents were not that perspicacious; instead they were lulled to an unquestioning gratification by the unique peace that had finally come to the Pengguling household.

Benign fate interceded, not only to salvage her plan from what would have been a demoralizing setback, but to hasten it along and help her see it through far ahead of her tentative timetable. Her savings had grown too bulky for their cache, so Maria transferred them one evening to the toe of a boot. Within a week of this relocation, Maria came home from work one evening to find that Grandma Pengguling—a veritable dervish of charity and domestic order—had gathered up all her "outgrown" toys and dolls and turned them over to the Salvation Army. Even the stalwart Maria was ruffled by the closeness of this call, but the fact that this crippling blow had landed clear of her, she said, certified the plan's eventual success.

It is by now quite obvious that Maria was plotting to run away. San Francisco or bust was her unoriginal motto. It was an alluring, ineluctable destination simply because it contained the memories and impedimenta of the most fertile, happy times of her life. Exactly how she would get there was an idea still relatively unformed, for she wanted her departure to be a clean and tidy masterstroke, hitchless and undetectable until she was safely in California. Her leave-taking must have style and cunning: she was not going to hinder herself by stealing away under the cloak of darkness with just a wad of cash and the clothes on her back, thumbing rides and being subject to every miscreant and reprobate that skulked the nation's highways. She would fly first class, but as it stood, she hadn't even her own suitcase, and was mulling over these maddening details when those random elements of the universe (if the reader will recall an earlier digression in this text) fell into line, and apodictic fate solved all her problems.

One day in that elfin month of April, while her region was still in the throes of a spring thaw, Cubby Pengguling, that vanishing whirlwind, departed on a month-long tour of France that she'd arranged. Within two weeks she'd telephoned home to inform her family that she'd fallen desperately in love with a Parisian businessman, was to be married there, and that her fiancé had generously insisted on bringing her parents and her daughter overseas for the connubial festivities. It was Cubby's desire that Maria be her maid of honor, in addition to helping her work out the final preparations. She wired money for her daughter's plane fare and some extra for whatever else she needed. Maria was to fly on ahead and get settled—for, of course, her mother intended her to live there—and her grandparents would follow in a week or so for the actual wedding.

Maria was flabbergasted by this stroke of exquisite fortune and even briefly courted the idea of actually going to France. But in her soul, she was still miffed over her mother's disinterest and absences over the last few years and chose to stick to her initial plan. After her grandmother made her plane reservation, Maria called in a reservation of her own for an earlier flight to San Francisco. Her grandfather drove her to the airport, while her grandmother, occupied with her own preparations, stayed behind. Maria, sincerely enthralled with these developments, had insisted they get to the airport with more than ample time to spare. Once there, Maria blurted with extreme agitation to her grandfather the question: of all the stupid things she could have done, what was the stupidest? Mr. Pengguling, a plain, good-hearted rube, guessed that she must have left her purse at home, complete with traveler's checks and all the other necessities of a young girl. He suggested that they send it right on after her or bring it when they came over, but Maria—lithe and statuesque in a trim, aqua linen dress, a lustrous aqua ribbon gathering up her voluptuous ebon hair—tamped her aqua patent-leathered foot in tearful consternation, stating that she would not move from that spot without her handbag, imploring him to fetch it for her, since there was still plenty of time before her flight departed, and promising that she would see to checking her bags and attaining her boarding pass in his absence. Mr. Pengguling, with the patience most often reserved for saints and novelists, kindly deferred to her request. What Maria had actually left on her bed was an old clutch that contained, along with other trinkets and tissues to create the illusion of fullness, a note explaining her motives, apologizing for her deceit and any inconveniences, and wishing everyone well. When her grandfather went off on the contrived errand, Maria cashed in her ticket to France, checked her bags for her California flight, and by the time Mr. Pengguling returned to the airport with the decoy, Maria was contentedly sipping a champagne cocktail and nibbling a brioche somewhere—thanks to good tail winds—over Ohio.

FOUR

"I f I'd spent any amount of time ruminating over my vulpine malevolence," she once said to me, "I would still be in Pennsylvania, pinching pierogi in the drafty basement of some church." (This author could add that he might very well be courting literary respectability rather than his current, silent obscurity, or at the very least a poetry chair at some educational institution.) I reminded her of France—as she attended to an inflating souffle, hovering before the window of our oven door like a wasp at its nest—but she was adamant that her honeymoon with Paris would have ended as soon as her mother's had begun, and that it wouldn't have been long before she was forcibly transferred stateside. Who knows?

In any case she touched down in San Francisco complete with clothes, luggage, and a lightness that even her understandable unfamiliarity with the city could not eclipse. Her first stop was the Tenderloin area in search of Mrs. al-Habim, but her mentor had recently moved on, so recently, in fact, that her apartment still held the ubiquitous smells of citronella and curry. The place was now occupied by an emaciated, virulent-looking man with splayed, tortoiseshell teeth, who told Maria she was welcome to share his abode for a few days until she found a place of her own. He matter-of-factly informed her that there was an extremely ill fellow across the hall who could go any day now, and so a place might be opening up soon. She declined with as much politeness as she could muster, but some of her revulsion must still have eked out, because the gentleman began to snarl and hiss as if he'd been terribly insulted, so Maria threw a fin at him and hotfooted it out of there.

As a very young girl, Maria had never had much of an opportunity to go beyond the bright and friendly rooms of her or Mrs. al-Habim's apartment, so the only real exposure she had had to this dire and impoverished neighborhood had been the occasional perspective from the fire escape, where the people who passed cigarettes from hand to hand, drank from mysterious bottles, and spent their days canvassing the sidewalks and stoops, did not appear so grim and sickly, so unclean and disadvantaged. If not for the familiar aromas of the apartment she'd just visited, she probably would have doubted her sense of direction. Standing on the street below, her primness making her feel obtrusive and uncomfortable, she looked into the mute, inarticulate eyes of a simian-faced boy wearing a tattered ball cap, and was riveted with a rising panic, despair, and pity ("the first bit of pity that I'd ever felt for anyone or anything besides myself.") Valiantly lugging her cumbersome bags, she began walking.

The next few days were spent in a hotel, where she conducted her search for an apartment. In just about a week's time, she responded to an ad requesting a female roommate to share a one-bedroom apartment in North Beach. She had found the cost of empty one-bedrooms to be prohibitive, not that she didn't have the funds for a few months' rent, but she felt that the less money she had to shell out, the longer she'd have to relax and get her bearings in her new city. The studios she'd seen had either been too small, or overlooked alleys, or had kitchens with barely enough counter space to dice onions without whacking one's elbows.

The girl with the vacancy was named Violet. She had lived there for just over two years, she said, and had therefore been spared the worst of the regular rent increases. The split, then, was enticingly low to Maria. The apartment was located in the corner of the building near the top of a hill. The windows in the living room captured much of the morning sun and from those above the kitchen sink, one could see a slice of the shimmering powder blue bay. Among its finer points were a double oven, a dishwasher, a mobile butcher's block to accentuate the already spacious work area, and a large, walk-in pantry for implements and foodstuffs.

Violet was a handsome enough girl, whom Maria guessed to be in her twenties (she never asked). She was tall, just over six feet, and seemed uncomfortable with her height, for there was a slight stoop to her shoulders, a compacted economy to her movements, as if the world around her were lilliputian, not designed with a slender, ambling girl in mind. Maria's unimposing stature (five feet, three inches in precious, bare feet: I measured her, and the bittersweet mark is still on my bathroom door frame) certainly contributed to Violet's delusion. She moved about the place with clipped, tiny, urgent steps and would stop abruptly at her destination, as if she'd reached the edge of an unexpected precipice or a hitherto unseen glass door. And then, having suddenly arrived, say, at the couch, she would pause, perhaps ascertaining that no unnoticed little people were imperiled with being squashed, and plop down. Her round eyes were ringed with a moist, rosy tinge, as if she'd been crying, but without the puffiness that results from shedding tears. This peculiar feature made makeup clotty and bothersome, so she went without it, leaving her eyes to their own pleasant color and, unburdened by cosmetics, open wide in perpetual wonderment.

Yet aside from her tall frame, quirky movements, and damp eyes, Violet's most outstanding physical characteristic was her hair, a long mane that Maria rates as the most beautiful head of hair she'd ever seen. It reached to the small of her back and was almost like gold, the soft and shimmering twenty-four karat of anklets and necklaces. It was a rich spun mass of filigree that so enamored Maria she could not refrain at their first meeting from asking to touch it. It was Violet's most enviable possession.

Maria recalled her first infatuated evening in the new apartment, while she was in the bedroom unpacking her things. Violet emerged from the shower, her naked body steaming and glistening pink, her hair darkened from the moisture but still as ebullient as that precious metal. Unabashed at being so thoroughly unadorned, she sat on the edge of the bed, the long sweeps of her comb extracting the excess moisture, her hair draped luxuriously over her breasts, her ribs, her belly. And Maria was mesmerized (an Absolute Moment), thinking she was in the presence of a Godiva or Rapunzel, a storybook incarnation, as Violet contentedly hummed and began the braiding process, certainly pleased that she was being so admired.

Maria realized that, up until this time, she had never had a legitimate friend, someone with whom she could interact without some façade to shroud an ulterior motive. Over cups of coffee that Violet enlivened with generous doses of Frangelico, they got to know quite a bit about one another, or at least Maria served up an unstinting portion of her past with fabrication, and only the most tasteful amount of ornamentation. Violet's history was not unlike Maria's: a variation on the bare-bones theme of parental inattentiveness, an unchanneled penchant for creativity, exploration and experimentation, a burgeoning need for autonomy, and the inevitable filial break.

Then having struck out on her own, Violet studied in the evenings, received her graphic arts degree, and finally got a design job in the publications department of a monstrously large bank, while still doing some free-lance work on the side with the hope of eventually starting her own graphic-design firm.

Violet assured Maria that, though she was "maddeningly self-reliant," she was not "greedy and domineering," but rather "a loving and titillating bunkmate, I think," who treated kindness with kindness. The vacancy that Maria filled had been created, said Violet—her eyes a bit glassy and glowing from the liqueur—by her "former slut of a roommate who had defected without warning" to take up residence with her boss in his Stinson Beach duplex, "where she perpetuates a cozy farce and pretends like she doesn't know me now." Violet got a bit tearful and sniffly, and Maria—a bit glazed herself—offered her sincere regrets, her heart going out to her new friend. Violet was grateful, said that she was already developing an affinity for Maria, and the friendship they were cultivating would help to melt away the cold disappointment she had felt for a time. Then, further emboldened by the alcohol, Maria went on to describe her plans and ideas, her unexplainable gravitation toward the culinary arts, her meager, early endeavors in painting and literature.

San Francisco, Violet assured Maria, was the best spot in the country for gastronomic apprenticeship, with the possible exception of New York, and her interests would be best served if she could find positions in places like Fournou's Ovens, Henri's, the Blue Fox, the Carnelian Room, or Ristorante Orsi. But without one iota of formal training, and only scant waitressing experience, this was next to impossible. Violet regretted that she had absolutely no connections in this area to even lend a hand, adding that the best she could do in way of assistance was to allow Maria total dominion over the kitchen, and offering herself as faithful guinea pig.

It behooves me to halt here and jump ahead to some vital information and further revelations to provide the reader with a more lucent understanding of Maria Perpetua's creative coming-of-age. *Spinacea oleracea*, while certainly not a whim, was also not a work independently conceived and realized, but was actually a sort of sidebar to something far greater, a magnum opus that has yet to see the light of publication and is certainly still being fired in the kiln of her scintillating mind. Upon moving into Violet's apartment and attaining the sought-after free reign, Maria realized that she lacked not only formal training for the pursuance of her culinary desires, but informal training as well. She had no idea where to begin. She knew the mechanics fairly well, but her tastes, notions and conceits were frenetic and unformed. As a writer stares at a blank page, so she found herself staring at a clean kitchen. In order to skim the coagulating fat from her rich ideas, she began her education by making notes to herself and, once trimmed, segregating them, so that each could be separately explored. Before she whisked her first roux or coddled her first egg, she already had a chronicle of thoughts and theories that grew with each passing day. This preambled her work and then complemented it as it progressed, until one day, as she was thumbing back through some notes on garlic, she realized that more than just random jottings, she had a sort of culinary memoir. Constantly adding to it, as well as refining it, editing it, clarifying abstract fragments, and excising unnecessary detail, she was building a work that she began to call *The Gastronomic Hejira*.

"When this work is complete," she said once in a rare admission, "it will be the bright, gleaming cherry atop the sundae of twentieth-century culinary literature." So it seems safe to assume that she intends to have published most, if not all, of *The Gastronomic Hejira* sometime before the year 2000. When I met her, she had upwards of half-a-million words with no end in sight. During the comity of our cohabitation, I continually urged her to begin preparing at least a first volume. What happened instead is history. A brief excursion into the realm of spinach grew into a protracted sojourn, resulting in her first and only publication to date.

Though I did not get to see any of *The Gastronomic Hejira*, I was privy to her drafts of an overture, or preface, to the work. Before she became engrossed with the idea and construction of *Spinacea oleracea*, she briefly toyed with my suggestion to prepare a volume of her ongoing work and wrote six or seven versions of a proposed introduction, of which she solicited my humble opinions. And it is from one of these introductions that I learned her appraisal of that critical time when she first moved into Violet's apartment and was ready to begin her work, the time she began the memoir and, essentially, her artistic journey. Because of her many versions, the one I purloined was probably never missed:

> I hadn't the vaguest idea where to begin. Imagine someone who fancies himself a writer: he carries with him the idea that he is a writer, he introduces himself as a writer, he speaks openly about projects, writing projects, he will soon undertake the moment he gets his own room, plenty of paper and ink, a good strong light. But he has never in his life written. He has only read the poems and novels of great writers, has marveled at their expertise and has patiently waited for his own chance to cut his teeth. But when he sits down, he finds that he simply cannot write. Why? Because he has never written a word of his own. He finds he does not know the first thing about writing. Reading has not taught him.
>
> Imagine me, then, as that young man, a writer who has never written, only read; I was a cook who had never cooked, only eaten. But I was even one step farther from such grandiose posturings. I had never even tasted the great foods I wanted to cook; I had only seen them in periodicals and cookbooks, had read how they were prepared and what they should taste like. I was like a writer who not only had never written a word, but who also had never even read the great poems and novels, someone who had instead acquired his dubious familiarity with literature from critiques, reviews and Cliff Notes.

She set about preparing her "reserves"—fish, beef, and chicken stocks, duxelles, minced garlic with a skin of olive oil, deboned chicken breasts—to save time during future experiments when she might not have long, full days to tinker. While cooking down stocks, a period to which she gave the rubric "preludes," she became apprised of some subtleties in flavor by various methods of cooking. While large bubbles of taste slowly rose and erupted at the surface of her broths, she sat about the kitchen table scribbling notes on aromas. And getting carried away, swallowed up in her own thoughts, she would allow a fish or vegetable stock to remain unattended for too long, letting it boil to an unusable bitterness. Or, in her preoccupation, she would neglect to scoop off a viscous layer of scum, or cover a bubbling pot too tightly, a circumstance that caused the broth to sour as it cooled. Her mistakes were minor, wholly illuminating, and never happened twice. These mishaps and her recognition of them were in no way revolutionary; she could have learned as much in any number of cookbooks. It was the learning process accompanied by a verbal record that was emerging as an altogether-unique bit of material.

Violet, meanwhile, seemed thoroughly delighted with the new goings-on in her apartment. She spent much of her free time there watching Maria cook or write, always ready and willing to dash out and pick up some light cream, a bit of gelatin or any ingredient that Maria should suddenly require. Violet insisted that Maria not hesitate to call her at work if she needed anything at the market, so that Violet might pick it up on her way home. Maria was at first a little leery and uncomfortable with Violet's altruism, but learned to take it in stride, accepting it as a gesture of their ever-improving friendship and as proof of Violet's claim to be a "loving and titillating bunkmate." After all Violet was being well fed, and Maria, being home much of the day except for her walks around North Beach for air and errands, did not ignore other household chores of cleaning, laundry and upkeep, though Violet would sometimes take a half-serious scolding tone and tell Maria that just because she did her work in the apartment did not mean she was a domestic, and that she should leave some of the tidying up for Violet to do on weekends.

Violet delighted in bringing home a variety of wines for Maria to taste and cook with, and imparting her admittedly sketchy knowledge of grapes and vintages whenever she could. Little of the wine, Maria remembered, was actually used in cooking: Violet always seemed to have a glass in her hand, especially in the evenings after work. While amending notes or making new ones, Maria would often look up to see Violet watching her with moist eyes over the rim of a long-stemmed wine goblet. Violet also had a curious habit when they were talking of reaching out and taking a smouldering cigarette from Maria's little hand, drawing deeply, and passing it back. Maria was tickled by this idiosyncrasy; it "warmed her heart," for it struck her as a kind of intimate bridge to their camaraderie. The grape she invariably shared with Violet also assisted in this warming.

Maria had a favorite illogical truth she would utter from time to time: that she was "more Proustian than Proust."* Each life experience, she believed, each defeat, achievement or oddity was tethered to the smell or ingestion of a certain food, a particular meal, made memorable by the surrounding event, and in turn, one needed only to duplicate these sensations of taste and smell to vividly reawaken the past. (Neural studies of recall functions base this method of remembrance in biological fact.) So it was one day, sifting through a mountain of notes, that she resurrected an early original menu, (*poulet au citrouille*— chicken breasts nested in a cucumber aspic, topped with a puree composed of fresh pumpkin, butter, nutmeg, and white pepper—followed by a pastry shell filled with fresh raspberries and garnished with a hot, rich Chambord sauce for dessert) and recounted for me the strange evening when Violet's cozy quirks and inscrutable, boozy euphemisms had become as pellucid as glass.

After the languorous and wine-accompanied main course (what the chicken lacked in distinctive flavor, said Maria, was made up for by the dish's pleasant, harvesty coloring), Maria returned to the kitchen to whip up her Chambord sauce. These long and talkative meals were the day's respite on those occasions when neither of them felt like trudging out into the night for a movie or a drink. Having earlier reclined in a simmering bath, Maria was padding barefoot about the apartment in her favorite at-home garb, a soft and roomy flannel work shirt she'd taken from her grandfather. Violet, in her silk, lotus-print kimono, joined her in the kitchen, lingering by the stove, sipping her wine and asking questions about sauce making. It was then, as Maria tipsily chattered about one of her theories on sauce (she believed that the brain apprehends the proper consistency, by registering the minute degrees of increased viscosity which, though almost incomprehensible to the eye, send signals to the subconscious), that she felt Violet's cool hand gently but confidently caressing her bare thigh. Maria was not so much startled as lullingly distracted. As Violet's patient, unforceful petting inched upward, her hand disappearing beneath the oversized shirt, the wrist of Maria's whisk hand went decidedly slack. By the time Violet's amorous, inquiring fingers

*For her more prolix explanation, see the introduction to Spinacea oleracea, pp. iv-vi.

curled beneath the lacy band of Maria's slippery-smooth bikini and drew it deftly down to no objection, the raspberry sauce was sweetly burning, bubbling unchecked, inedible and utterly forgotten.

It is impossible to say how keenly Maria shared Violet's sapphic proclivity, though it is safe to assume that she was not entirely averse to this type of physical love, or their subsequent string of feverish, lusty tumbles would not have taken place. Her first seduction was the result of pure, heated desire; there was nothing calculated in Maria's eager consent. From the initial contact she was overcome by a craving to have her body liberally explored and excited by a gentle and informed partner. And when the steamy tête-á-tête had been seen to its mutual spasmodic conclusion, and Violet was softly breathing in sleep, her golden hair spread thickly across the pillow, Maria slipped out into the kitchen and attacked her journal with a new and breathless ferocity, intensifying her cogitations by occasionally bringing the tips of her fingers to her tongue and reawakening the heady flavors of their ecstatic repast.

Maria realized that first night that to have rejected Violet immediately or, even worse, to reject her future attempts at affection, no matter how graciously, would poison their relationship, probably causing their living arrangement to become increasingly insufferable until Maria would have to move. Even if the situation did not turn overtly harsh, it would still most likely have produced cold underpinnings, and a growing insensitivity on the part of both girls toward one another's creative sanctum sanctorum.

Maria recognized that this was altogether unfair; logically she had every right to fend off Violet's advances and still expect a harmonious relationship, since, after all, Violet had advertised for a roommate and not a lover. But urges are impervious to logic.

Maria is not the type to be one-upped. If she could not control a certain situation and use it to her advantage, then she would flee. I cannot report with any accuracy—since Maria was misleading and nebulous on the matter—whether her decision to stay stemmed from an attachment to this facile habitat that was conducive to her work, or from a certain depth of affection for Violet, but I'm inclined to think it was a little of both. Maria had surreptitiously decamped and made it all the way to San Francisco with ridiculous ease: she could surely have found a new apartment, or a new roommate, and set up shop elsewhere without much problem. Whatever her reasons for staying, one thing is certain: her remaining in that apartment, in that affair, was predicated on her manipulation of the circumstances. She made as many demands for affection and sexual subservience as did Violet to allay any appearance of being a kept woman, a pretty, pusillanimous plaything. Violet became, as unwittingly as the woeful Joe, another muse.

This was not without its drawbacks. Maria's commitment to their illicit affiliation and her vigorous, unashamed pursuit of pleasure caught Violet unawares; for the first few days the older girl was anxious and jittery, perhaps unnerved by the extraordinarily passionate monster she'd unleashed. Maria admitted that she had come on a tad strong after their first encounter, though her wanton behavior was as sincere as it was theatrical. After one meal, as Maria was clearing away the plates, Violet innocently asked what was for dessert. "Grapes," said the insouciant Maria, who then hopped up on the table in front of her friend, bunched up her flannel shirt, and proceeded to dribble Violet's sparkling wine over the glistening curlicues of her dark, pelvic pelage. Poor Violet was so startled and overcome that she began to weep hysterically, and Maria had to help her to the couch and comfort her, stroking her sumptuous mane, cradling Violet's sobbing head against the sticky bouquet of her lap.

Violet tearfully admitted that evening that she had never had a lover of either sex who was not her subordinate, in fact who was not slavishly submissive to her (for she did indeed enjoy an extremely rare bit of intimacy with men, but only under very select circumstances of her own devising, usually, she said, when she was feeling inexplicably lewd and perverse). Maria's aggressiveness had shocked her; she did not know how to react to it. Thus her emotional outburst. They talked it over. Violet felt better. Their discussion, coupled with Maria's tacit resolution to be a bit less brazen, brought things to a more tranquil pitch.

This atmosphere of calm lasted a goodly stretch of months. During that time Maria continued with her writing, though she didn't look upon it as anything other than exercises and reflections, a catharsis for her kitchen activities and the unknown direction in which they were taking her. She followed this merry path with her receptors open wide, with her metaphorical feet unshod, in the hope that somewhere along the way she would pick up some distinct thorn of thought, some cocklebur of reason that would imbed itself deeply and garner her attention. She searched so desperately for that singularly splendid tile with which she could make her debut that she failed to see the entire, sublime, Byzantine mosaic that was spreading out around her.

When she wasn't cooking or writing, she spent the balance of her time with her roommate (whom she'd taken to calling Ultra-Violet since, in the crucial moments of bliss, that girl's ululations would soar into the upper register before disappearing into that tonal realm that was audible only to dogs), either whooping it up around the apartment or cavorting between their favorite points of local interest. The corners of Maria's mouth would inch and flutter into a near smile when she recalled these excursions. With pints of Italian ice they sat on the cool spring beach and silently watched the Pacific, listening to the eerie, yelping barks of distant sea lions, the hiss and thunder of collapsing waves. They took the window table on the upper level of their preferred Chinatown restaurant, surveyed the street through the smoky glass and ate chow fun and pork buns and a wonton soup that was chock-full of various sea creatures. They lingered long at an open café on Columbus, where the cappuccino was unmatched, and the patrons curious, eclectic, chain-smoking with affectatious manners and animated, inspired outfits that captivated Maria. They packed into Violet's Honda for Saturday jaunts to Napa, and Sonoma, shuttling from vineyard to vineyard, tasting the wares and toasting the prolific grape (about which they exchanged bawdy, inside jokes in reference to Maria's now-legendary tabletop ablution).

One afternoon they found themselves in Jack London country, and stopped at a rustic, isolated café called Wolfhouse, where they ate open-faced crab sandwiches and drank bottles of Heineken. Maria recalled this day distinctly, for they fell into conversation with the only other customers, a fivesome who were tight from an afternoon of wine tasting and very communicative. In the exchange of pleasantries and small talk, Maria found that they were all recently transplanted Pennsylvanians and had all come from the same general area where Maria had spent so many dismal years. She was flippant in her remarks, a bit cutting, and though it didn't seem to trouble her new, temporary friends, it had a strange, creeping effect on her, filling her with an unexpected melancholy, for she began to say that she had family back there but caught herself. It was the first time she had called upon herself to summon up a piece of unhappy, intimate history, and all those years of resentment, discomfiture, of time biding, woolgathering and duplicity that had led to the ultimate schism, constituted a dark and hostile abyss. There were no feathery pleasures to fall back on, except for some vaporous early memories of San Francisco; no incidents of satisfaction to dwell upon, except for the dubious "success" of her scheme. This brief, desultory meandering through her short past yielded nothing, no fond scraps or opulent baubles that she could turn over in her hand, polish and examine.

But these blue, fruitless forays for artifacts and relics were uncharacteristic of Maria. She steered away from maudlin remembrances, for at that point in her life, she mistakenly equated memories with nostalgia and sentimentalism, two interchangeable states of mind that she quite correctly knew to be dangerous. Her own return to the Tenderloin had taught her that the lost days over which we lament are illusory, that we alter and abridge them to suit our present needs and exigencies; they become the tenuous superstructure upon which we build, and when we return to find that these memories in which we've invested so much are merely fictions, these mummified foundations crumble into dust from the fresh air and harsh light of reality.

So then, in the days of her second muse, she was steadfast in avoiding what she called "The Land of Wot-Wuzz" and committed heart and soul to the exploration of "The Land of Wot-Iz." A total refutation of the past, however, is as self-defeating as a morbid preoccupation with the future.

Life changed. Violet grew unhappy. The transformation was gradual, and Maria, so smitten with "The Land of Wot-Iz," might have noticed had she taken the time to pay more than an obligatory amount of attention to her partner. The accretions of countless meals and ever-present food began to blur the lineament of Violet's once slender frame. In order to spend more time in the company of her love, she resigned her full-time position and concentrated her efforts on free-lancing. Maria, fearing a blight of finances, made a token gesture at finding a job, but Violet strictly forbade her from doing so, convinced that she should not interrupt her work. Besides, Violet had sacrificed her steady salary so that she might keep a tighter reign on Maria. Though Violet had always expressed a desire to be professionally autonomous, to secure her own bank of clients and be her own boss, her move was prompted more by insecurity, ironically, than confidence and forthrightness. The faithful Maria had never given her any reason to doubt, but still Violet was becoming covetous and possessive. As her figure puffed and billowed, her self-assurance fled. She became slothful, sullen, and developed a host of psychosomatic maladies that plunged her into greater depths of inactivity and self-pity. She took to spending long hours in bed, the victim of debilitating spells and ambiguous pains, with cold compresses draped across her forehead and hot-water bottles wrapped to her abdomen. Maria spent an increasing amount of time tending to Violet's agitated whims, fetching aspirin for her one minute, thawing out chicken broth for her the next, only to have Violet reject it because she was overcome with swells of nausea. Violet became stiff from remaining supine for too long, and Maria was obliged to knead the muscles in her back, to braid her hair because Violet said her fingers were feeling gnarled and arthritic. At the height of one of these negligible illnesses, Violet woke one morning with the idea that enemas would be the proper panacea, and after a few hapless, messy flushings (Maria was thoroughly set against it and refused to assist, hoping that would dissuade her, but to no avail), the lethargic Violet was forced to spend another seventy-two hours in bed before she was strong enough to get up and move about again. She dropped some of the extra weight she had gained, but the reduction was disproportionate: her face became haggard and pallid, her hair lost some of its luster. For the first time her usually sharp, adroit manner of locomotion disappeared and was replaced with a kind of feckless shuffling.

One morning, as Violet readied herself for an appointment with a new client, Maria walked into the bedroom and found her at the dressing table unskillfully applying eye shadow to conceal her sickly, darkened hue. Violet smiled at her. Maria managed to dredge up a smile in return, but she shuddered at the scene: Violet seemed to have aged three years in three months. Despite this, however, Maria tried to convince her that these cosmetic amendments were entirely superfluous, that she did not have to resort to artificial enhancement, if only to start Violet back down the road to her former nature of self-possession. Violet assured Maria that this was the lone exception, that she wanted to look as bright and ebullient as possible for this one engagement. After that all these paints and potions would go into the trash. Maria asked for Violet's promise, which she got. Such superfluity would be all right this one time, but Maria didn't want her to make a habit of it. Thus, garnering Maria's approval in this way, Violet perked up immensely. She was eager about her meeting with the client, whose account would be a boon to her free-lance business.

Maria watched as Violet began brandishing a pair of tiny tongs with a clamp whose curvature conformed to one's eyelashes and lent them a smart curl. As she was squeezing down, poor Violet's excitement perhaps got the best of her, for when she lifted the device from her eye all of her unfortunate lashes came with it. Not quite certain of what had happened, she gave herself a hard, puzzled look in the mirror and then broke into a volcanic burst of tears, thoroughly rent with embarrassment, broken, and utterly demoralized. It was a terrible setback.

The full, sobering effect of Violet's dystrophic decline finally dawned on Maria. She devoted even less time to her work and more time to ministering to her friend, trying to reinstill in her that old spirit, plying her with vitamins, encouraging her in her design work, but the notion that she might soon have to find a way out of the relationship was gathering weight. Even Maria, when pressed for explanations, admitted that she really didn't understand what had happened, but in hindsight, she said things would have been better had she left them alone. Violet's distracted, mournful quality and intermittent bouts of irrational jealousy were bothersome, but Maria could live with them. This moodiness changed, however, during her rehabilitation, and Violet became more argumentative. She seemed to be envious of Maria's work, or her ability to keep at it so diligently. She misread Maria's increased attentiveness as a ploy to placate her suspicions about infidelities and assignations that did not exist. And when Maria shifted gears and was not as fawningly gentle and conciliatory, Violet thought she was being spiteful, and enacting a sort of emotional blackmail. As so often happens in affairs that are just not meant to be, behavior that was once cherished and accepted as proof of undying devotion when the relationship appeared utopian and permanent is suddenly viewed as reprehensible and malicious. In Violet's metamorphosed scheme of things, Maria could now do nothing right. And it was this disgruntled demeanor and petty paranoia that formed the fulcrum for Maria's departure.

FIVE

I n the interest of history, I have tried to be as objective as possible in my reportage. To achieve this objectivity, I have often had to ponder naked details and speculate on the unspoken emotional and psychological factors that rest at the bottom of this shallow pool of information, and give Maria Perpetua the benefit of the doubt, assigning her more compassionate and humanistic qualities than she was wont to admit. Thoroughly disregarding my misfortune in my personal dealings with her and sticking with her own sparse statements, I would have found it far easier to paint a portrait of a heartless, parochial artist, a selfish, spoiled savant. She seemed to derive a certain satisfaction from assessing the impact of persons and events in her past with utter indifference (i.e., "She was unimportant; I just used her," or "That means absolutely nothing to me; it was all an act to get my way"), as if she wanted these cold dismissals to crystallize around her, to make her a precocious princess sealed in ice, unexposed to the trifling intrusions of an irksome world. She wanted to appear hard and clinical, or perhaps she actually fancied herself hard and clinical, though I tend to doubt it. This phlegmatic aura in which she enveloped herself was betrayed by her regular moments of tenderness toward me and the genuine joy and intrinsic goodness that epitomized her prose. Nothing mean spirited or dissolute there: her writings had the glowing and intoxicating life excitement of the paintings from Cubby Pengguling's Prenatal Period.

Aside from that, the very act of trying to convince me of her general misanthropy seemed in itself at least a partial denial, a vain groping for her as yet nascent identity. Consider this analogy. By way of striking up a conversation with the gent jouncing next to me on a cable car, I mention a television program I viewed the night before. My neighbor snorts with contempt. He does not watch television. He considers it the vice of addled asses. I assure him that though his opinion of the practice has some validity, all that flickers is not foolishness. I wouldn't know and couldn't care less, says he, and begins to vigorously ignore me. I detect the odor of falsehoods and self-deception. How can he have such a vehement disregard for something about which he admittedly knows nothing? Chances are, my neighbor spends his evenings in television's dim blue spell, watching bawdy comedies and gargling Budweiser, instead of sipping Earl Grey and sampling Emerson, as he strenuously hopes his friends fancy him doing.

So it was with Maria and her exaggerated attempts to unsettle and convince me of this callow mien. If I should ask her, "Didn't you think about how you would hurt her feelings?" she would briskly reply, "Who cares about her feelings?", a dismissal of such automatic contempt that it just did not ring true. In my humble but not entirely uninformed opinion, I believe that these grotesque reactions were the products of a little guilt and a lot of wariness. I believe she cared, and was confounded by such simple humanity, such simple kindness, uncertain of what function it had in her ongoing invention of herself.

I am not suggesting that Maria, despite her insinuations and admissions to the contrary, possessed at her core a blinding and providential monstrance of virtue. It is true that some of her maneuverings were executed with the dispassionate precision of a hired killer. But these murders were for sustenance, not profit; above all else her creative life was sacred, and even the prospect of causing someone serious emotional trauma and heartache would not deter Maria if she believed her work was in danger. Her irreverence toward compassion and the human condition actually acted as an insulator not only for her, but for me. Such preparation and awareness was supposed to soften the ax blow of separation when it came. Out of love, appreciation, and a twisted kind of consideration, she was doing me a service.

All this is flapping, broad-winged psychological nonsense, however; it buffets the air but does not bring flight. One may claim that the luxury of hindsight illumes the dreaded particulars that heralded the souring of a situation, and that, had we affixed them with a more discerning eye at the instance of occurrence, we could have recognized then what we recognize now. But I take umbrage at such a ridiculous notion: hindsight, like nostalgia, is illusory. We give weight to ambivalent, ethereal events in order to rationalize and justify our pain; in our craving for order, we lend logic to illogical acts and unforeseen moments. Though it would be a trenchant and tidy piece of reasoning to say that, on that sultry April day, against the enameled backdrop of an azure bay, my offerings of food and drink were an ominous precursor of the endless flow of unanswered sustenance I was to give this girl, it is nevertheless unacceptable. That grand and elusive perspective is the stuff of fiction, and we would be better served by avoiding the pat packaging of that smarmy realm.

And so, with her tulle veil lifted back from her face, she drank the thimbleful of beer in one swallow, drew her tongue in a provocative pass across her front teeth, said she felt like walking and blithely asked if I would like to join her. As there was nothing else in the world I would rather have done, we set out for an indolent stroll around the wharf, engaging in relaxed conversation full of unanxious pauses and thoughtful ellipses, the bulk of which—except for one or two fossils in exquisitely uneroded relief—is extinct in my memory. Words are subordinate; actions are the building stones of confederacy. She slipped on a pair of white-framed spectacles with round, red lollipop lenses and fixed her tinctured eyes on me, as if asking my approval of this fashionable accessory. She stopped at a vendor's table and considered some silver and turquoise bangles, and a gold-plated arm band cast as an asp with two blazing peridot eyes. Suddenly we found ourselves in the atrium of The Cannery, where a crowd had gathered to watch a stilt-supported entertainer in immense pin-striped trousers juggle Indian clubs. With a calf love whimsy that makes us suddenly attach untold value to mundane objects, I bought her a valentine-shaped foil balloon, which she diplomatically gave to a little boy whose face had cherry smudges from the candied apple he was urgently gnawing.

She asked me what I did besides selling seafood.

"I am . . . self-employed," I said cryptically.

"Is it lucrative?"

"Hmm, that depends," I said. "Let's just say that it yields some very gratifying profits, not necessarily monetary."

"Now there's something," she grinned and fell silent, letting the subject flutter off unpursued.

Thus began our inscrutable courtship, over which I had very little control, though, of course, I did not realize this at the time. My vain delusions had me convinced that, since I was the intense object of her desire, I had reign over the elaborate proceedings. She would sometimes shadow my daytime movements. While at work I would turn and glimpse her down the street, watching me from a block away, standing amidst the audience for a street performer. And when I would turn back the next instant to ascertain if it were actually she, she would be gone. Other times, when my keen eye did not notice her anywhere and I assumed she was not around, one of those tricycle cabs would stop behind me, and the driver would hop out, slip a note in my apron pocket, and drive off—a note asking me to meet her at a certain location later in the day. And on other occasions, when I would neither see her nor receive messages from her, I would recognize her up on that tavern's balcony, dressed in blue jeans and an oversized cable sweater with the sleeves bunched up above her elbows, leaning against the rail and staring out toward Alcatraz, the late-afternoon sun burning red off her spectacles. I would then run to catch her there, to surprise her—thinking that her vigil had been interrupted by a moment of dreamy distraction, and I had spied her before she spied me—only to bolt up the steps and through the bar to find the balcony vacant but for the old black gentleman who gathered empty bottles and cleaned the ashtrays. Maria would then turn up, perhaps an hour later, in a flouncy dirndl and a provocative linen camisole blouse with drooping, vermicelli-thin straps (drawing my attention to the smooth white disc of a vaccination scar on her shoulder which I longed to anoint with a moist and amorous kiss). She would assure me that this was the first time she'd been out that day, adding incredulity to that former image, causing me to doubt the veracity of my eyesight and to wonder if the presence on the balcony had simply been a mirage, a projection of my smouldering ardor. As I said, I did not realize it then, but each apparent chance encounter was predetermined by her; each casual sighting of Maria observing me from a distance occurred because she wanted me to spot her. With this type of reinforcement, she embroidered herself in my consciousness in such a fashion as to make me believe that she was always in the vicinity, always on the verge of showing herself or making her nearness known.

It was during those days that the confidence and amusement I felt from the notion of being the focus of a young woman's infatuation began to dwindle and disappear and were replaced by a fain longing for her physical presence and a mania for locating her in episodes and areas where she could not possibly be. Thanks to the stirrings of this obsession, my every waking action was under the scrutiny of this fata morgana. As I composed in the solitary lamplight of my apartment, she was there just beyond the rim of incandescence, gazing piquantly at me with an approving eye. She cooed and marveled at how intensely I meditated over my sheaf of papers, how elegantly I scraped away the morning's whiskers, how impeccably I folded the hospital corners on my Murphy bed, how pensively I sipped my coffee and turned the crackling pages of a book. Only through considerable concentration could I banish her back to her wispy realms, as when I visited my quaint and fetching Yvette (for Maria and I, despite our increasing number of rendezvous, had not even shaken hands, let alone kissed), and even then her specter would swim up through the murky haze of passion, and I would confuse the climactic, dulcet pipings of my handicapped harlot with the enflamed oohs and ahs of a phantasmic voyeur.

Poor Yvette could not help but notice the change that had come over me. Our usually talkative sessions were now filled with generous silences; we were bobbing on a raft of stark physicalities, and all around us, like an immense and endless ocean, was a great, soundless void that swallowed me when our carnal maneuvers were concluded. As if I were the only person in the room, I failed even to greet her, to acknowledge her presence. After our swift and wordless coupling, I sat sullenly on the edge of her bed in just my stockinged feet, staring at a nightstand clustered with the candles she liked to burn when I visited, and watched milky, molten wax drool slowly down their shafts. She touched my shoulder and recoiled—I was cold in more ways than one—asking me what was wrong, and I gazed at her with, I am sure, the eerie, vacant eyes of a somnambulist. Out of disgust, bitterness, and confusion over my unsettling, uncharacteristic behavior, she did something she'd never done before. She slipped out of bed, hobbled to the door and switched on the overhead light—something that is disturbing for its harsh, ugly brightness, its blanching, penetrating intrusion, to someone who has spent any amount of time in gentle, mutely lit surroundings. We squinted at one another: Yvette standing by the door, unclad, her deformed foot bent at an angry angle and audaciously plain; I equally bare, perhaps paler and, like Adam, suddenly convulsed with shame, as if the unflattering light were the rebuking voice of the Creator. And we shared the terrible recognition that things had changed forever.

My mind and body were racked with lovesickness, one of life's most beguiling and indescribable maladies. The vigor of this affliction, the stimulating chemicals it seems to release in us, and the twisting it creates in our entrails when we try to act on these incitements, creates such interchangeable states of agitation and inactivity that the afflicted often appears to be under the ebb and flow of narcotics. One cannot allow this state to remain unattended for very long, since the risk of inflicting some permanent damage becomes greater; mad, inspired damage to one's physical self (e.g., Romeo and Juliet; Young Werther; Van Gogh sans ear), or worse, a kind of mutilation of the soul which dogs one through the rest of his days, particularly when he is aware of the sickness but fails to act on it. This is not to say that outright protestations of love and blatant attempts at possession are cures; they are not. At best these medicaments remit the symptoms but do not destroy the disease.

People often ask, "Do you believe in love at first sight?" as if such a thing were a supernatural phenomenon or an extraterrestrial encounter, something entirely theoretical since there is no documented evidence to support such a belief. Many will answer "Yes," not necessarily because they believe in it, but because it is a quaint, fantastic thought, and it is entertaining to consider the possibility that there is something new and inexplicable under the sun. And yet, though God may indeed be in His heaven, devils may be setting up shop in the bodies of little girls, and ghosts and Martians may very well be capering about, "love" at first sight is as ridiculous a notion as the flatness of the earth. The gaze of strangers can sometimes connect in some arbitrarily fatal way, and under proper conditions with the right moony demeanor, the space between them will be charged with particles of interest and attraction. With enough of these particles and a willingness in both parties, these two may very well get together and enjoy a relationship, sometimes an eternal one. Then, in their procrustean and love-drunk imaginations, they will recall the mutual sighting as "love at first sight."

Far be it from me to throw cold water on these two, but they are simply the victims of man's perpetual estrus, and not the beneficiaries of some cherub's intangible arrows, as cozy a thought as that might be. "Love"—if I may pick up where centuries of philosophers, poets and women's magazines have left off—is a state so labyrinthine and complex, so contingent on trust, integrity, moral resolve, and innumerable other elements that are impossible to glean from a glance, that it simply cannot spring full grown into being, like Athena from the forehead of Zeus, as a result of the enamored look of two strangers on a crowded subway train.

A favorite theme of these romantic fictionists, once they are past "love at first sight," is "love against all odds." These love affairs usually consist of a pair who are, by dint of background, ideals, or social acceptability, thoroughly incompatible. Any degree of rational thinking informs them that they are so diametrically opposed that a love between them cannot thrive. Yet (and this is why these things are called fictions), they buck the system of reason, the intransigence of reality and live happily ever after, or so it is implied. What they don't bother to explore is, though the idea of opposites attracting may be intriguing romantic fodder, and the adventure of something so illicit is the fire that keeps our protagonists burning for one another, it is not an eternal flame, and the two are doomed unless one compromises. And in these strange affairs, one usually does. When lovesickness is rampant and crippling, one person (most often the weaker, since the affliction creates more inner havoc for him and causes him to do things that he would normally never consider) forms a cathexis to the other and gives himself over unstintingly. For the sake of L-O-V-E. (This transformation, then, completely negates the original idea of forbidden love, of love flourishing thanks to alluring adventure, since for the love to continue, the adventure must abate.)

You may say, "Yes, my good man, you are absolutely right, this is just a lot of hokum, but, like small children believing in Santa, it is relatively harmless." Not so. This instantaneous, freeze-dried love and the cosmic compulsion we attach to it are the virulent organisms that spread quickly into lovesickness, and lovesickness, while making for good picture shows and gothic fiction, does not make for good life.

When I saw Maria that first day on the wharf, I did not know it then, but the germ was in the air and I inhaled it. Our—

nay, her—subsequent cat-and-mouse games served to give it a warm, moist place inside me and helped sustain it. By the time of my ugly rupturing with Yvette, I was convinced that our affair was unavoidable, that there was a mystical inevitability taking shape and that to deny it, not to vigorously pursue it, was madness on my part. Forces much greater than I, I reasoned(?), were working the levers. Who am I to quibble with celestial manifestos?

There was the danger. After these few weeks of innocent meetings, I still knew comparatively little about her, yet in my eyes the bond was ordained. Our relationship was a phatic one. She expressed no hard ideas, intentions or philosophies that might convince me a viable and long-lasting liaison was plausible, but simply maintained an air of conviviality that gave me little reason to doubt it. I was hooked, damn the torpedoes. If someone had approached me and said, "You know, she is a fascist," or "I hear she poisons children," the information would have bounced off me like bugs off a windshield, and I would have responded with trembling voice and aching heart: "Love is not love which alters when it alteration finds, or bends with the remover to remove." If we can't trust Shakespeare, whom can we trust?

The idea that an undeniable bond existed between us was further strengthened by her timing and understanding of these forces at work inside me, though it was probably more a logical comprehension of the natural course of my emotions, the emotions she twisted and pulled like taffy. So thoroughgoing was her game plan, and so deft was her execution of it, that she preempted my hard-fought and painfully achieved resolutions to intensify our relationship. She anticipated an affectionate comment, a longing look, a declaration of love. This occurred so naturally it gave me the eerie feeling that she read my thoughts and knew my motives.

I waited for her on the tavern balcony early one splendid evening, teetering on my chair's two back legs, one elbow upon a weathered, peeling windowsill, the other hand holding a sepia bottle of beer, and idly contemplated the comings and goings on the wharf. Running over and over again through my head, on a perpetual loop, was a winding, protracted admission of devout and urgent love, filled with assurances of fidelity and sincerity, with tangible testimony to my puzzled and purblind state, with the sweet and unsullied purity of my affection for her and my conviction about the mutual happiness that would result were we to become tender and informed lovers. So constant, rapid, and overlapping were these declarations that from time to time I had to whisper my prepared speech aloud in order to untangle the springs and coils of heartfelt words. Behind the cityscape the sun blazed low and orange, bristling and quivering brightly through the irregular geometry of buildings, like flames reflected and rereflected amidst an arrangement of mirrored boxes. Charles, the rumpled black custodian, occasionally milled about, perfunctorily wiping condensation rings from the tables, and collecting and carrying away empty bottles by sticking them on the ends of his fingers, as many as eight at a time (his thumbs were too fat), so that his hands looked to have some exotic disease that left him with grotesque, distended digits. Once or twice my whispering penetrated his reverie and I peripherally noticed him stop, bent over a table, and cock his head to one side like a curious puppy, trying to pick up a bit of my quiet conversation and ascertain if it were directed toward or in any way concerned him. Finally he asked, "You be talkin' to me, sport?" but I just cleared my throat and shook my head, not bothering to look at him, unwilling to take my eyes off the people below. He paused next to my balanced chair, looked into the crowd to see what could be so riveting as to command my rigid attention, then shrugged his shoulders and went inside, the ossified growths at the end of his fingers butting and tinkling like chimes.

My tentative, impatient spirit was sinking with the sun. The scattered clouds, like tattered scraps of cloth, were darkening, scudding across an early, gibbous moon. The orange light was replaced by a crepuscular purple and dirty pink. I believed that if Maria had intended to see me that evening, she would have already arrived, unless she was trifling with me, seeing how long I would keep a vigil for her. But that thought was spawned by my melancholy, and I did not entertain it very seriously. All my pluck and words, already a vaporous, ephemeral construction, would have to be reserved, perhaps for another twenty-four hours, a discouraging proposition. They began to disperse and collide due to the beer I'd been drinking, and spoken repetition no longer kept them intact but instead, like sugar heated and spun into sweet filigree, dissolved them the moment they reached my tongue.

Convinced I was not to see her, the tautness of my determination loosened, the numbing, careless effect of the alcohol swarmed over me, and I began blinking hard, trying to ameliorate my fuzzed, smeary vision. I did not relish the thought of walking home and was poised, on two spindly chair legs, between that endeavor and the desire for another beer, when I heard the brisk tattoo of someone rapping on the window behind me. I swiveled my lightened head, and there in the window was Maria, a thinlipped, slyboots smile on her face, with enough crumpled butts in the ashtray to indicate that she had been sitting there for some time. I furrowed my brow and looked at her for a few boozy seconds (figuring it was another in a long line of plaguing apparitions) until she said "Hi!" There was no confusing the crispness of that one sharp word with hallucination. Shocked and flummoxed by suddenly being in her presence, my tenuous balance was disrupted, my chair shot out from under me and, legs and elbows flying, I plummeted to the floor with a walloping crash.

There is a remark (courtesy of Robert Burns) about best-laid plans invoked so often that one would think that we, the foolish living, would realize how futile it is to prepare remarks and cast ideas in the unreal vacuum of our brains. Life is too mockingly contentious to stay any course, to follow any pattern, to conform to our naive notions. But our persistence in such blunders is the quality that separates us from the rest of the world's species. Whatever remained of what I had wanted to say was decimated by my fall. As I got to my knees, trying to compose myself, rubbing a bruised coccyx, Maria rushed to my aid, suppressing her laughter as politely as possible, brushing the soot from my palms and straightening my spectacles.

"Why were you just sitting there?" I asked, gathering myself up.

"Darling," she said, "I just wanted to watch you a bit, that's all. I wasn't playing tricks," and contritely widened her eyes, though she needn't have done so since, in my perfect estimation and strident need of her, my forgiveness would have been just as automatic and irrevocable had she said she was waiting for exactly the right moment to slit my throat. Then, bending close to my ear, her words thick and warm with liquor, she breathed, "Take me to your apartment and I'll *cook* for you," and took a bit of my ear lobe in her front teeth.

Even as I heard clanging pots and clattering cupboard doors while I washed up in my tiny bathroom, I was still under the impression that her suggestion was for something else entirely. It was only when I'd emerged in a clean cambric shirt and a splash of flowery cologne, and found her standing before a stove topped with steaming vessels, clutching two mismatched plates and a handful of woeful, mangled eating utensils, that I realized her offer had been a literal one.

"I don't understand you," she said. "You have a variety of cooking implements, but practically nothing to eat with."

"My mother gave them to me," I said. "And I don't entertain much."

"I suppose not." She turned back to the range and eyed the babbling goings-on. "And I don't see a table anywhere. Just where do you eat your meals?"

"I usually stand over the sink," I said sheepishly.

"Why don't you clean your things off that desk and we'll eat there?" she said, handing me what she was holding.

I shuffled papers and piled texts, corralled an errant pencil stub that was rolling away, trying to escape the herd. Thinking that this arm's-length romance would have to continue as such, only this time over plates of hot food, had blunted my passion somewhat. Her attention was held now by her simmering melange, and I simply stood by, trying to look pleased and hungry, my self-confidence evaporating and my tastefully fragrant *odeur d'amour* put to shame by some intoxicating, buttery shallot substance she was delicately folding with my heat-resistant spatula.

What I did not realize (for if I had, I would have been flattered and enchanted and far more relaxed with the way the evening was progressing) was that by cooking, Maria was making love to me; it was her sparking song, her courting lyric. Gastronomy, its fact and theory, its act and appreciation, was her superlative expression and greatest gift. It had reached the plateau of high art for her, and she did not parse it out to just anyone, but only those she held in the highest esteem. As she said to me somewhat earthily a few months later, "Anyone can [be intimate with] anyone else, it doesn't take much effort, imagination or affection. Devotion is sharing your greatest possession, your highest and most prized Level of Being." (Sometime much later, when an inextricable wedge had been driven into our relationship, I widened the fissure with a mean-spirited comment to the effect that I was not aware that being a self-aggrandized scullery maid was a higher "Level of Being." In my sour memory, that remark, whatever its instantaneous impact, was not so much a poisonous touché as it was the inward-twisting tail of a scorpion bent on stinging itself to death.)

The buttery shallot substance was a satiny Bercy sauce of such subtle, artful elegance that I gasped upon tasting it. Certainly, I said, she could not have composed it from the capricious and anemic foodstuffs that I had in my schizoid bachelor's kitchen, but she assured me she was not a conjuring witch, nor had she smuggled in any ingredients in her purse. A meal made from my supplies was a challenge she was by now equal to. She had currently delved into a mode of cooking that had several apropos labels, among them "Exploiting the Chaff" and "Turnip Blood," until she had finally settled on the more refined "Minimalism." The Bercy sauce, she said, was "the epicurean's equivalent to haiku," and though not her own recipe, it still bore her signature with an added "Teutonic lilt of coddled caraway." She draped this custard-colored master-piece over some baked chicken wings which she had carved free from a block of ice in my arctic frontier of a freezer (I use the generic "baked" for lack of a better word, for she had a classified method of preparing poultry that extracted every last drop of flavor from "the chemically glutted birds of twentieth-century America" that she would neither divulge nor allow me to witness since, she maintained, every cook and food *auteur*, like the master illusionist, has a secret or two that keeps his or her actual work ever superior to even the most thorough, to-the-letter disciple and emulator. The method remained a mystery, and we used to refer to her fowl as never being baked or boiled or broiled, but "Perpetuated."). And this all rested quite comfortably on a bed of . . . spinach, what else? We did not know then that we were feasting on our leafy green fate. There were also a small side dish of noodles—"store-bought," she crinkled her comely nose—with tarragon butter, and glasses of beer. As there was only one desk chair, I dragged my coffee table across the room and sat on it, which left me several inches lower than Maria. This immediately put me at a conversational disadvantage and threw me into another crisis of confidence, for there is something incontestably ridiculous about a grown man at eyeball level with his food.

I had never given much thought to my eating habits until that time. I was meticulous in observing what little etiquette I knew, though due to my peculiar seating arrangement, I had every excuse to throw etiquette to the wind. (I was spared from my common habit of propping my elbows on the table, since it would have required a hyperextension of muscles that would have been excruciating and unendurable.) I ate slowly, took only a modicum of food on the uneven tines of my sad fork, chewed carefully, and even set my utensils down between bites, affecting a thoughtful, appreciative mastication, smiling and shaking my head in a kind of delighted disbelief over the stellar meal. I commended her effusively after nearly every mouthful; so effusively, I fear, that my sincerity became somewhat suspect. She rebuffed my compliments by saying it was nothing time and again, and time and again I assured her that it was much more than nothing, it was indeed something (basing my encomiums on a comparison to *my* culinary ineptness and not her far superior abilities), until she leveled a stern look at me, circumflexed her eyebrows and said with a cross finality, "It. Was. Nothing. End of topic," at which point I cowered behind my pile of denuded chicken bones and assumed the meek comportment of a disciplined child, for which I was so aptly seated.

To rekindle the dinner's rapprochement, she then detailed the depth and breadth of her vocation. At first she spoke cautiously, prosaically, with the trepidation of one who is unwilling to describe the extent of her feelings for fear of being considered hysterical or absurd. Upon realizing that my interest was honest, since I did not smirk, or yawn, or show any other condescending signs of humoring her, she became less matter-of-fact. Her speech intensified, her words tumbled forth effortlessly, breathlessly, as if she was thinking aloud rather than talking, and the utterance of those thoughts was a method of snatching them before they fluttered off, like fireflies captured and contained, glowing evocatively in the crowded density of a jar. And like the pulsing phosphor of a firefly, a soft light seemed to flicker in her eyes, the light of one possessed by what she says instead of simply saying what she possesses; a light of fervor; not external light reflected but an internal light emitted, projected through articulate celluloid and focused on me, the screen. She talked about food as metaphor, food as subtle control and blatant tyranny, food as currency, food as a foundation for memory and art, food as the root of revolutions and societal shifts, food as the object of worship, compulsion, food as narcotic, food demonstrating disdain, homage, empressement, food as penance, as booty, food, food, glorious food. She overwhelmed me. My head was beginning to swim as that word was repeated so many times it lost its connotations and became a meaningless puff of air. I reached for my glass but she stayed my hand and held it fast. Her trajectory steepened, and she became visibly agitated. She talked of nuances of taste, texture, of bonding disparate elements, of the disappearance of some food types ("as extinct as dinosaurs and dodos") and the evolution of others. Her gush of words, laden with anecdotes, allusions and other obscure scholia, became less and less intelligible to me. She leaned urgently across the table; her speech accelerated. She gripped my hand tightly. Her cheeks were blushed and ruddy.

"Food is the literature of nature," she whispered hotly, her face just inches from mine. "Vegetables are adjectives, spices are action verbs. The knife is the quill, the plate the page. One fine bouillabaisse is Emma Bovary's heaving bosom."

I tried to pull away but couldn't; one of her nails broke the skin of my wrist.

"Maria, let go, you're hurting me, dear."

"It's pride and prejudice, status and subservience. The egghead, the rapscallion, the old salt, the spaghetti bender, the cheese eater, the meathead, the cute little tomato, the cream puff, the hot dog, the ham, the nut, the vegetable, the fruit! Let them eat cake because they drive a lemon but bring home the bacon to the apple of their eye who's one smart cookie and cool as a cucumber!"

"I can't bear it!"

"Think of the hope it gives, the cruelty it inflicts," she said, one knee now up on the desk. "As punishment for Tantalus, the gods placed him up to his chin in a pool of water that receded each time he tried to drink, and the trees bent low," she grabbed an uneaten chicken wing and held it before me, "and taunted—tantalized—him with succulent figs, splendid apples, pomegranates, and pears. Each time he tried to eat . . . ," she paused; a drop of cool, jellied Bercy pulled free and plopped onto my lap. I made a lunge for the wing with my teeth. ". . . The Zephyr blew the branches out of his reach!" she cried and with a snap of her wrist, flung the chicken across the room, where it splatted against my bathroom door.

"I'm bleeding," I whimpered.

She was atop the desk on all fours, catlike, her back arched.

"Adam and Eve and the forbidden fruit, the unleavened bread, manna from heaven, loaves and fishes multiplying, the fatted calf, the Lamb of God, the Body and Blood of Christ . . ."

"What does that prove?" I yelled. " 'Not by bread alone does man live!' "

" 'But by every word that comes forth from the mouth of God.' But do you think they would listen to that God if they didn't have anything to eat, if they didn't have food in their stomachs? What does that prove!" She released my hand, and I jerked it away. My wrist bore a series of crescent indentations, one of them welling up with a meniscus of bright blood.

"I mean," I said somewhat more calmly, "what are you saying? You've lost me."

She suddenly seemed to realize that she was crouching amidst our meal and gingerly retreated, careful not to redouble her embarrassment by sinking her knee into the cold spinach, or pressing her palm into the few oily noodles that remained on her plate. She creaked back in the chair and swiveled a half circle away, tucked a black curtain of hair behind her scarlet ear, showed me one blushing cheek. I was silent, gently sucking at the tiny laceration on my wrist, waiting for her to continue. But my response had broken her trance and she seemed disconsolate, grimacing slightly, as if all the ideas just voiced had seeded a humiliating cloud that was raining back on her in cold, freezing drops.

"Please, Maria," I said, "go on. It's okay."

"I can't go on," she said.

"You certainly can. Honestly." I modulated my tone, trying to sound as if my wits were sufficiently gathered.

"I can't work in a vacuum. She's insufferable. She thinks that *I* depend on her."

"Who?"

"But I need someone to bounce ideas off. Or else my insides get horribly knotted, and I don't know if I'm following the proper course."

"You can bounce ideas off me," I said.

"You're sweet," she finally turned toward me, smiled weakly, then said, "Could you help me find a new place to live?"

"I already have," I ventured rather warily, unsure if I should ask for fear of being rebuffed, then on an insuck of breath, half asking, half stating, "Here?"

"You don't know what that means. I don't have a job. I'm not earning any money from my work."

"All the more reason," I said confidently, certain that I now had her (not realizing until much, much later that those preceding weeks she had worked to elicit and accept such a proposal, and that she had me. O, love is such an eyeless, groping creature!). "How can you live on your own if you have no income?"

"I could get a job," she said, pride sharpening the edge of her voice. "I'm not some . . . some tapeworm. Some parasite . . ."

"I know that," I smiled. "But nevertheless, once your work has found a groove, don't disrupt it, don't derail it if you don't have to. See it through. This is your chance. Don't think that my insistence on your living here is entirely altruistic, my dear. I'm . . . I'm . . ."

Her eyes rounded in expectation; she bestowed one dilatory blink on me, one long softening look as I sat there openmouthed and adolescently addlepated.

"I'm . . . still bleeding," I said, nervously bringing my wrist to my lips. "I'd better get a bandage," and rose to go to the bathroom. As I stepped around the desk, she stood up in my path and took hold of my arms. I had just enough presence of mind to remain silent, immobilized by her tender, brilliant eyes (two glazed globes of hand-painted ceramic) and receive her full, slippery, luxuriant kiss, so passionate and probing that a minute, high-pitched, ecstatic sigh formed in my throat and popped with all the frail resonance of a gossamer soap bubble.

"I can't live in a place that doesn't have a bed," she whispered. "You wouldn't happen to have a bed around here, would you?"

"Hidden discreetly," my voice cracked, "in the wall behind you."

"Think you could unfold it when you finish bandaging yourself up?"

I nodded quickly and scurried off to the bathroom where my heel crushed down on Tantalus's chicken wing, which sent me rocketing across the linoleum with such velocity I would have skated for quite a distance had the sink not been there to catch me by the midsection, relieving me of every last ounce of air in my lungs, and leaving me prone, gasping asthmatically, on the floor.

She lit candles. I had a variety of these misshapen, scented things sitting around atop the orange crates I used as end tables. They were the cheerless, glutinous relics of salad days with Yvette, who had made a present of each of them over the course of our meetings, and they had sat cold and unused for several weeks. The guttering flames and redolent perfumes filled me with a steely, prodding remorse that I would have preferred to do without. I had intended to throw them away for some time and though that was something simple enough to do, I'd never managed it. From the days when I had burned them regularly, they remained a corpus of callous reminders, each uniquely deformed.

And now they flickered again, much to my chagrin, though I didn't care to explain to Maria why I would have preferred the humble darkness. With all of them lit, the atmosphere was a chorus of aromas, of lilac and hyacinth and lemon and pine, each contributing to the peculiar, schizoid smell with none dominant or singularly recognizable. The air seemed both heavy and coarsely dry. Our shadows were black amoebas, hyperbolic and grotesque: trembling, swelling and contracting in such a monstrous way that they appeared to be the source of the unnatural sounds that emanated from our raucous bed. When in the company of Yvette, the freakish flux of these great swatches of candlelight had given our couplings a dangerous, erotic ambience, but that evening, with Maria, the feeling was cruder, more pagan and ritualistic.

In those moments, however, I didn't think too much about such things, but instead surrendered myself to the placid, generous lassitude that washed over me as I lay back, Maria's head upon my shoulder, her extravagant, tar-glossy hair splayed over and around us.

"Will you come with me when I collect my things and move out of there?" she asked, braced for a battle she did not wish to fight.

"Of course," I said. "You didn't think I would expect you to do all that alone."

"It's not the physical work. I haven't very much," she said as if she were proud of that fact. "It's the emotional dirty work. I don't care to bear that burden alone. It might be unpleasant."

"Who is this girl? Is she dangerous?"

"Ultra-Violet. And she's only dangerous if you're extremely susceptible to great globs of self-pity. She'll certainly be slinging them around. Unless we get lucky and she's not there, but she's always there anymore."

"I don't understand. What's the problem with this . . . what did you say her name was?"

"She is just a sad, embittered girl who perceives me as her mistress, and will probably view my leaving as an affront to her desirability and personality. The girl who lived there before me moved away to live with a man. The poor girl will be a crushed and tattered Violet, but there is not much I can do about it. That's the way these things go."

"*Were* you her mistress?"

She was scratching light, tickling lines across my chest with the lethal nail of her index finger.

"We shared moments of mutual comfort," she said.

"Ha! What an answer," I blurted unintentionally. She caught my nipple between her thumb and forefinger and twisted it. "Ow!"

"Don't tell me about vagaries, mon ami," she said. "'I'm self-employed,'" she aped my words from our very first walk together so many weeks before, though her tone had a tweaking, moronic exaggeration to it. "Anyway," she continued, "does it matter much?"

"No," I lied. The fact that she might equally enjoy the

company of women was not disquieting to me because of any peculiar sexual connotations, but because the chances of her companionship being plundered from me had suddenly were doubled, since I feared her head could be turned by the female segment of the population as well as the male. I came to find, however, that mere mortals, whatever gender, were no cause for concern.

"You're troubled," she nevertheless observed, "but you needn't worry, mon ami, because I'm a devoted little thing, honestly I am, and no one's mistress but Art's. And vice versa. I need only comfort and understanding and . . . ," she swung a cool bare leg across my hips, "inspiration. Come on, now . . ."

"What?" I played dumb as she nuzzled my ear.

"You have gallons of inspiration," she hissed. "Give a little."

"You're kidding. Again?"

"I was just limbering up those first two times, sweetie."

"Maria, I've had a pretty harrowing day—"

"Oh, I *know*," she said sympathetically, "with all those nasty falls you took because of me . . ."

"They *have* taken their toll—"

"But you're a poet. And an epic poet at that, not just some clever mediocrity spinning out doggerel. You climb mountains, you achieve new heights." She took playful bites at my ribs.

"Yes, but—"

"You reach pinnacles that normal men cannot even see, lofty hidden places in the clouds," she trailed off, her words giving way to rapturous, maddening kisses.

And I succumbed.

The next day was Saturday, the opening of a new and momentous chapter in both our lives, with Maria as the self-appointed, auctorial presence. She had not intended to spend the night in my digs, but an understandable fatigue had over-taken her, and she slumbered soundly in my embrace until morning. Several times I considered arousing her, but figured that she had been aroused enough for one evening and, upon awakening, might prefer to traverse the ground we had already covered, rather than be escorted home, wherever that might be. Into a new day, after a sleep of dreams seasoned by the prior evening's spicy denouement, I was more inclined to take up where we had left off, but Maria, invigorated more by the dawn and its unlimited, creative prospects than by my tremulous, urgent caresses, leapt out from my canoodling attentions and readied herself for her subsequent "defection" from Violet.

As I folded up the Murphy bed, and snuffed out the few remaining candles that had not been drowned in the flood of their own molten wax, she pulled open the bathroom door and spoke to me from her dainty perch atop the commode, water crackling briskly beneath her. The horseshoe seat, she said, was "hideously cold."

"When we've breakfasted," she continued without a hitch, "I'll take you to meet Ultra-Violet, the poor girl." Whenever she spoke of her former lover and roommate, she always, from then on, referred to her as "poor," "sad," or "unfortunate," as if Violet had an illness eating interminably away at her.

"I'm not particularly hungry," I said. "I could do with just some coffee for now."

"Believe me, mon ami," she blotted herself delicately with a puff of scented paper, "you do not want to supplant my cooking with a simple, unnourishing cup of coffee," the flushed toilet an exclamation point. "The first thing you take into your body in the morning is very important, helps the tone. Those 'coffee-first-thing' people think they feel rejuvenated, but they run down quickly. Besides," she pulled her hair back and secured it away from her face with an elastic band, "I'm at my damndest in the a.m. My meals and ideas vibrate with vim and vigor."

Freshly scrubbed, she prepared that vigorous breakfast, which was the prototype for a long line of eggs Florentine (for some reason I had an abundance of frozen chopped spinach. "Insipid stuff," she said, "but it'll do in a pinch.") with the emphasis, or vibrato, this time on the hollandaise rather than the potherb.

Her hollandaise was almost to the point of constancy and perfection; she had prepared it often enough that she could nearly do it without looking, the way a musician might play idle scales without consciously realizing it. Eggs Florentine then, for her, should have been a lark, a child's composition, a nursery poem. But she had the grave handicap of having to rely on reconstituted lemon juice instead of the real thing, and a slight, but understandable, exuberance with this ingredient made the pale, sunny sauce wincingly tart, completely smothered the flavor of the egg and gave the spinach (that had already sacrificed some of its edge to the freezing process) a peculiar, rotting taste. Such tartness, even when expected, creates an involuntary spasm that is impossible to mask or suppress, and when she came from the kitchen while I was in midpucker, I knew it would not be a pucker lightly taken. She pounced on her plate and took a quick mouthful, exhibited the selfsame facial distortion and, amid a barrage of expletives, threw down her fork in disgust. After some shushing and palliative words, I managed to calm her down, and suggested that we postpone her move for another time, believing (if the importance of the morning's ingestion was what she claimed) the bad taste that had constricted our lips perhaps augured a potentially acerbic and unpalatable day. But the failed meal only fomented her determination, convincing her that not yet being thoroughly free of Ultra-Violet was clouding her creative faculties, and that if she could soak in the bathtub a while, she would resume her composure and refocus on her fixed purpose.

Basking in a near-blistering bath had become one of her artistic idiosyncrasies, a meditative preface to work where, she said, the mercurial albumin of her ideas was poached to a more palpable cogency. (She would spend so much time submerged during our cohabitation that it became necessary for me, after periods of cloacal patience prolonged to the point of pain, to invade her steamy think tank and sit while she stewed, an immodest arrangement with which I never grew comfortable, though I've no doubt that kings and presidents would throw modesty out the window if it came down to soiling themselves. Maria recognized my prickly embarrassment over this, and when she felt a bath coming on, would say, "If you're going to go, go now," but you can't just manipulate the hands of your internal clock to suit your needs.) So she simmered and splashed, meditating and occasionally muttering to herself behind the closed door, which still bore a frozen sunburst of congealed sauce from the previous evening's airborne wing, while I busied myself with a kitchen full of dishes, gulped down a couple clandestine cups of instant coffee, and contemplated why I wasn't as demonstratively joyous as I felt I should be, considering the last twenty-four hours' turn of events. Perhaps the full scope of the occurrences hadn't yet sunk in or had been tainted by the hollandaise.

When she finally emerged, rubefacient and hot to the touch, we set off for Violet's apartment. The fog had not yet burned off, and the morning was still drenched in that familiar gray and drab mist, as if the moisture that had insinuated itself into each crevice and around every corner had absorbed and synthesized all color from the city's surfaces. One needed only to be out for several moments, it seemed, before also becoming neutralized and imperceptibly immured into the chiaroscuro, the somber shading of that forties film *noir* atmosphere. The sun was only a cool white disk in sharp, discernible outline, a bald, craterless moon. Saturday shoppers filled the streets, autos jockeyed for precious parking spots.

Maria did not seem to notice or acknowledge much of the life humming and honking around her. Her hair, pinned up by invisible black clips, bobbed about her head with each strong stride; her tiny, protuberant chin was pressed forward in firm resolve; and her eyes were dark, icy spangles of unwavering will. So forthright and fierce was her look that passing pedestrians glanced at her and, in what must have been some defensive reflex, stepped farther aside than was necessary to let her pass, hoping to remain clear of whatever wrath it was that so solidified her features and animated her locomotion. At a sidewalk espresso bar, a gaunt-faced black man in a faded dashiki and a tiny silk fez fixed her with a prolonged gaze over the top of his foreign-language newspaper, an inquisitive look in his round, onyx eyes, as if trying to imagine what injustice she was out to avenge, what violence she was bent on enacting. I, too, had to keep a close eye on her, and not become too immersed in observing the busyness of the buzzing street, lest she make an abrupt, unsignaled turn and leave me continuing straight on ahead. I made some inconsequential remarks about the dankness, the chill of an occasional swirling breeze, but she treated them to a simple "humph," indicating to me that there was a time for noting external trifles, and that time did not happen to be now.

She turned a corner, stopped sharply before a beige brick building and inserted a key into a dinged, brown security door. On the wall inside the elevator-sized foyer was a bank of mailboxes, and as Maria attacked the next door that opened onto a corridor, I scanned the tin gray fronts and found, on a slotted panel numbered twenty-four, "Webb, V., Perpetua, M." I bent down and peered at the names, as if close inspection might yield an illuminating clue to the awaiting mystery. Maria, whose agitated celerity had caused her to fumble and drop her key, stooped to retrieve it, and in doing so, butted her enticing rump against my protruding one, and I knocked my forehead a brilliant thwack against the cold steel with enough force to jar open a number of the small metal doors, causing a variety of missives and magazines to tumble out onto the floor.

"What are you doing?" she gave me a queer look, gripping the key so tightly the skin beneath her thumbnail went white.

"Nothing," I said, trying to gather up the fallen items.

"Leave it." She finally pulled open the second security door and started ahead. "That's a federal offense, you know," she said in a voice too stern to be joking and scampered up the stairs.

Violet must have heard the confused thud of our footfalls in the second-floor hallway, for she was standing in the open door clutching a cup. She was taller than I. Her florid kimono was slightly askew and loosely belted so that the front was open in a deep V, revealing the soft bone ridges in her chest, her smooth, epicene lack of cleavage, and the even, fish-white plane of her belly. When her slit eyes caught sight of me, her bare front swelled full with a deep breath and then slowly receded. Her golden hair spilled everywhere around her, some bunching in the collar of her robe, some stuck beneath the belt and gathered at her hip. Much of it appeared frizzed and brittle, with errant strands kinking and radiating off in different directions like the crinkled spikes of a corona. There was something unsettling and witchy about her disheveled appearance, as if she were a descendent of Macbeth's conjuring triumvirate.

Whatever comment she had prepared to assail Maria with was lost in her befuddled surprise at my presence. Not giving her a chance to retrieve it, Maria took the offensive.

"You look horrible, Violet, simply horrible. Excuse us, please."

Violet stumbled back a few unsteady steps, still gaping at me, an uninvited freak of nettlesome nature. I meandered in and made a cursory look about the apartment, though all I could see were Violet's wet eyes staring at me.

"What . . . what," she stammered, "what is this?"

Maria came from the bedroom with an armful of dresses.

"Really, Violet, you're so rude. That, if you must know, is a poet."

"A . . . a *man* poet!"

Despite her innocuous coffee cup, the camouflage of its true contents was betrayed by the deliberate slowness of her speech, as if her words were bits of food lodged in her teeth, and she had to extract them with the tip of her tongue before spitting them out. When the full implication of that lucid bit of detective work suddenly dawned on her, she clasped her robe shut and began wailing to the ceiling, "It's happening again; O, I don't believe it's happening again!"

"Nothing is happening, Violet, so just quit yelling." Maria returned dragging one bulging suitcase. "He is just going on a trip for a few weeks and is kind enough to let me use his apartment as . . . as a *pied-à-terre*. I have some important work I want to get started, and I need to give it my full concentration and attention."

"What can you get there that you can't get here?"

"Peace, Violet. Peace. It's just a brief, solitary, artistic sabbatical."

"You're lying! You're taking all your clothes, your things! Why are you taking all your things if you're coming back?"

"Violet," Maria placed a small fist on her hip, "I don't have that many things and I will need all of them." Maria turned to me, as if suddenly remembering that I was in the room. "Mon ami, why don't you just sit down on the couch? I'll be another minute or two."

"I don't feel like sitting, thanks," I said warily. The tipsy Violet was already looming closer, and I did not want to give her a further advantage should she decide to pounce on me. In addition my tailbone was throbbing from the prior-evening's pratfalls.

Violet held her coffee cup in both hands and drank down the contents. Fortified, she cleared her throat and shuffled toward me.

"Just what are you, really?" she said. Her breath bore the scent of some cordial. "Are you some kind of born-again?"

"Young lady . . . ," I inched backward until my calves were against the coffee table and there was no place to go but up.

"Or are you just one of those studs who go around taking in dykes and deprogramming them? I'll bet that's what you are, huh? Stud?" The word was encased in a bubble of moisture and as it broke from her lips, a bit of spray hit my glasses. It was the saliva that caused me to flinch, but Violet—unfortunate, inebriated Violet—believed that it was the force of her questions.

"That's what she is, if you didn't already know. She likes other girls. No, not other girls; this girl. Me," and her lower lip, dry and finely cracked, began to tremble.

Intense emotional turmoil and alcohol are a volatile admixture; I no longer feared that she would assault me, but that she might become physically sick on me. I weighed the pros and cons of standing pat or retreating to higher ground and decided to take to the tabletop. Lifting one foot behind me, I stepped up. My ascendance steered Violet out of her impendent swoon, and the image of me towering over her—a superior position, as if she were the deposed queen in some sexual *coup d'état*—angered her.

"Wha'd you do, give her drugs, give her cocaine? That's probably what you did." She put her bare foot on the edge of the coffee table but it slid off and thumped to the floor. "That's probably what you did, you scum. And now she needs you, she needs to stick with you to keep up her habit."

"I am a poet," I hopped down, not caring to risk another one of those calamitous falls that had been occurring with alarming regularity.

"So?" she challenged.

"So . . . poets don't use cocaine," an asinine declamation if I ever heard one. What I'd meant to say was most poets can't *afford* cocaine, but it probably wouldn't have mattered anyway. Violet had finally scaled the table—her head skimmed the stuccoed ceiling—and, with both hands on her hips, was rocking her upper body back and forth like a metronome. "You should come down from there," I said.

"What! What did you say to me?"

"Violet!" Maria emerged with the companion suitcase. "Get down from the coffee table!"

The willowy girl reeled back slowly and made a soft, dusty

landing on the sofa. Satisfied that Violet was safely grounded, Maria hurried off to the kitchen with me in pursuit, not wanting to be left alone with sad Violet again. She began taking plastic containers and small parcels wrapped in aluminum foil from the freezer, and putting them into a brown grocery sack.

"You're taking food!" Violet shouted from the living room. Deep into the sagging sofa, her knees level with her eyes, she struggled to extricate herself from the cushiony recess, and was having a devilish time in her apparently worsening condition. As she was rocking forward, trying to propel herself up with jerks and heaves and groans of effort, her robe slipped down her shoulder and a pretty, pink-tipped breast nudged its way around the lapel, like the squirming nose of a kitten one might have concealed in her jacket. I turned away, flushed and despairing, wishing I hadn't come along.

After more bumping and thumping that Maria and I ignored, Violet finally said in a restrained, quivering voice, "You're taking my food, Maria."

"Violet," Maria stopped packing and looked at her. She was now erect, standing in the middle of the living room, her robe clasped tightly and her arms folded fast around her. "Violet," she said testily, "these are soup stocks and reserves and other preparations that you *know* are mine. I prepared them. Besides, what in the world are *you* going to do with beef suet? They belong to me."

"You're taking my food," said Violet evenly. "I bought it. I paid for it; it's mine. I don't care what you did to it."

"Mon ami." Maria looked at me and spoke as if she hadn't heard a word of what Violet had just said. "If you should happen to be staying with a friend, let's say, and your friend loans you his pen, his ink, some of his paper, a desk to write on and all, and you, using his ink and paper, write a batch of poems, who would those poems belong to, hmm?"

"Of course they would belong to me, but . . ."

"Of course they would belong to you," she turned and glared at Violet.

"Of course they would belong to him," Violet shouted, flapping her arms at her sides (and I half expected her to leave the ground, a great, golden albatross), "but it's not the same thing!"

"It is unquestionably the same thing," said Maria through

her teeth and slammed the freezer door. "Now if you could get the suitcases please, I will take this sack and my notebooks."

I carried the two bloated suitcases into the hallway and waited for Maria to say good-bye. She pulled several loose-leaf binders from the floor of a closet, double-checked to make sure nothing had fallen out or been left behind, and with her armload of books, planted her diminutive self directly in front of Violet. Maria was nearly a full foot shorter than her friend, who was staring vacantly, hypnotically at nothing in particular, her head tilted slightly to one side.

"I've left all my utensils," Maria said gently, deprecatingly, "so you see, I'll be back." Then she put her hand on Violet's shoulder, stretched up on the point of her toes and kissed the tall girl ardently on the mouth.

Violet sat down weakly on the coffee table and was still glazed with that same dumbfounded, bovine expression when Maria finally closed the door behind her.

With the two weighty bags in tow, I struggled after Maria for a block or more before she pointed out that the suitcases had tiny casters that simplified their transportation. With the ugly deed completed, the return trip was not as rushed; her pace was markedly slower, her countenance more benign, but for the most part, she was still incommunicado. Nevertheless, as we trudged and jostled along, I treated her to a small lecture on the improper analogy she'd made to Violet concerning the foodstuffs.

"They are not the same thing at all, my dear, not at all. I can write poems without paper and ink. The writing is all here in my head," (the cutting handles were still burning the skin of my palms), "but you can't make chicken stock without chicken. You can't prepare duxelles without mushrooms. You can't retain a bouillabaisse in your brain."

"I know that perfectly well, mon ami. I should have compared it to an artist and his canvas, a sculptor and his clay, something that takes more physical dexterity and talent." I grimaced. We were stopped at a corner, waiting for the walk signal. She looked me over with a quaint, amused smile.

"You were moved by her pitiful attitude. I know," she said. "Me too."

This admission caught me completely off guard, and I nearly asked her whether or not this were true, since it was certainly not apparent. But when I turned to her, she was staring back out across the street, as if considering the immensity and terrible grandeur of some ocean, with that earlier look of resolution: that slightly jutting chin, those glittering, dark eyes.

"Like all liars, I just said the first thing that came into my head. But some things just must be done," she said, and cleaved her notebooks tightly to her bosom.

SIX

Things must remain unspoken since I cannot see
Myself singing the utter unutterability
Of it all. I am a great showy creature flapping noisily
His widespread, earthbound wings of impotency;
Yet the dust we've raised, the whirling, funneled swell,
Stings my eyes and makes me choke and gasp for air,
And act in ways good sense could not foretell,
Since in life good sense is singular and rare.
And if the ensuing events were plain,
I'd keep my thoughts, myself, to me,
And suspend the actual, anxious pain
In the amber of safe reverie.

It is the curse of the human condition, amidst all the
incomprehensible stuff and incredible nonsense of daily life, to
have a few fulgurant, lucid moments. We marvel at the cool,
detached, sensible perspective of our minds. And once we have
sufficiently admired our big bright thoughts, we boot them
down the nearest empty stairwell, where they lie crumpled and
forgotten until some pain has been inflicted, some indignity has
been done, at which time we stumble upon them again, sitting
forlorn, neglected, but as clear-eyed as the day they were born.
Then we clasp them to us like a forgotten child, as if our strong
embrace will work retroactively, or give us the clemency we so
desire but don't deserve.

In the days prior to the consummation of our cohabitation, I composed that sonnet with others in the throes of one of
those rare moments of providential clairvoyance, rational fore-
sight, common sense, or whatever that invisible beast calls
itself. The future I strained to visualize was shadowy and
inchoate, and rejected any concrete features I affixed to it:
Maria and I in five years, content and domesticated, picking out
material for drapes; Maria and I crouched side by side attending
to a garden, our knees cold and musty from wet soil, our fingers
sticky from weeds, a graying crescent of earth smudged across
her rufous cheek; Maria next to me on some dais as I accepted
an award or movingly read a poem, her hands folded, her
approving look mantled with pride and beatitude. These images are the spots and squares and motes of colored light that
impinge on our eyesight as we read, that dissolve and fritter
away when we try to hold them in the center of our vision. In

71

those moments I was visited by the "utter unutterability of it all," and filled with the leaden and saturnine notion that life's most desirable circumstances and ideal arrangements are such simply because they are so unattainable.

But these isolated cogitations were as brief as steam. They were shoved aside by my immediate yearnings: all surrounding time, life, and landscapes were blanched and robbed of color and relief, and I was alone, an impassioned poet in a void occupied by nothing but my own need for one particular gratification. Possessing, or being possessed by Maria (whatever the case might be), was not just something above all else, it was all else, and only after this had come to pass could I throw open the casements of my soul and flood the world with its former hue and texture. Once that has happened, I would think—postsonnet and past midnight, an iridescent lump of hashish intensifying as I sucked deeply on a rosewood pipe— then we'll consider this murky feature; we'll lift up the crumpled figure at the bottom of the steps and scrutinize it closely, check for some physical resemblance, ask it some pointed questions, try to ascertain if it is really our progeny or just a silly imposter.

So, if I would not heed the intermittent tinnitus of reason and suspend my torpor in that poetic lozenge of amber, I would follow my heart, as they say, and assuage the temptations by giving in to them. Whatever should follow—guilt or giddiness, pain or pleasure—would at least be in some way edifying, and would rid me of the muddled and immobile state of mind that consumes one who constantly dances on the fringe of desire, neither willing to thoroughly ignore it, nor to vigorously pursue it. I waited for the warm and purling swell of tranquillity to anoint me. It never did.

I had her. She was in my home, a happy, humming adornment that had finally arrived to fill the space that had always existed for her. And now her presence, which I felt would surely plug my gushing incoherence and otiose ponderings, instead opened a Pandora's box of rude paper snakes and flash-powder foolishness.

She would emerge from the tub and wrap herself in the raiment of a pale pink towel, a tinted crêpe, with its darkened rose continents of moisture, her skin soapy fragrant and waxy as isinglass, and I would hurry to close myself in that tiny room and inhale the humid essence she had left behind. As she worked in the kitchen, I would pretend to be reading, while all the time listening to the various clinks and whacks and blurbles of her procedures, the components of some cryptic code that might quiet my thudding heart if only I could decipher them. And when she would suddenly enter the room, wagging a ladle or champing on a pen like a flamenco-dancer's flower, a furious pounding would rise up in my chest—a beating that threatened to burst free or crush itself, like the desperate exertions of a bird one has captured in his hands. I would observe her from the corner of my eye, my throat clogged with an inexplicable compunction, as if I feared she might have learned of some dark, imaginary secret of mine, but would not reveal the extent of her knowledge, so that I must microscopically examine her movements, the bends of her expressions, the register and rhythm of her voice to determine whether this vile truth had infected her. She would wordlessly locate whatever she sought and creep felinely back to the kitchen on the soft balls of her feet, careful not to disrupt the placid meditation of my seemingly deep thoughts.

For those first weeks she was lovingly meticulous about keeping my habitat free from any disrupting elements, any unnatural intrusions that could alter the chemical balance of my poetic hothouse environment. She remained as unobtrusive as possible, imperceptibly assimilating herself like a nature photographer who sits unthreateningly still in the presence of chimpanzees day after day until they accept him as just another unremarkable member of their band. Had it been anyone other than Maria, I would have continued to rhyme and reason as always.

Though I believed that she truly appreciated my companionship, cherished my solicitude, respected my intellect, opinions, and sensitivity to Art (meaning, not my understanding of a solitary work of Art, but my comprehension and deference to the Nature of Art: its demands on the artist, on society; its mysterious workings; its tyrannical demeanor), and probably even felt a sincere, unsophisticated physical attraction to me, something was still sorely absent; something eluded us (or me, more likely): a comity of our spirits; a hybrid, mutual soul; a duality that the closely intertwined share; a cosmic vista from which they view the world as one entity. Distinct from one another only in terms of body, they absorb life through one combined set of eyes, filter it through the cheesecloth of one essence, and when this distilled impression is spoken or set down on paper, one could very well sign both names to it, since it would not have been gleaned and interpreted in quite the same fashion had the writer been alone on his cliff, gazing down into the remote chaos.

Or perhaps this amalgamation did exist, but was of unequal portions. Perhaps Maria's creative spirit, rich and fecund, overbearing in its fullness, simply stunted and squelched my own in this combination of essences, and my paler faculties shrunk from the light of her intellectual fire. Perhaps I literally loved her to distraction.

What else can explain my terrible lack of lucidity, the pitching and lurching of my thoughts? As I sat at my desk, my brain all clear sky and warm, supple levanter, a phrase would begin to sluice forward, a thought would billow and blow taut some sail, and I would begin to cut through a placid sea of cornflower blue, one confident hand on the tiller, one eye following the morning sun, when suddenly all types of cerebral hell would break loose. A wash of words and abstract, inarticulate swells of ideas would crest and crash with sonorous, biblical fury. The mainsail would go flaccid and clap like a baseball card in a bicycle's spokes; the useless rudder would tear free from my grip and thrash like a compass needle in a magnetic field, and without warning I would be in the dire Strait of Messina, listing violently from side to side until I was spun and capsized and mashed against the rocks. Nothing would remain, no written log, no proof of any poem's existence, save for a jagged word or two which would buoy to the surface, now swirling meaninglessly, unseaworthy, and unsalvageable. How could this occur time and again? Whence did these tempests come? They had to be Maria's, yes, I know it: they were the turbulence from the tumid clouds that engorged and purpled her thoughts. I know it.

She wrote standing in the kitchen, curling close to the page, supporting herself on her left elbow, her weight on her left foot, the other leg bent and gently swinging at the knee, soundlessly tapping her toe off the linoleum. Spread out before her were graying, dog-eared sheets of lined paper, notebooks, index cards rubbed raw with erasures. Her head tilted slightly to one side, she would regularly lift her pencil, as if at each comma, and use the butt end of it to draw her tumbling, meddlesome hair back behind her ear where it would remain through the next burst of scribbling, then fall free once more, and she would brush it back again, a habit that was as natural and integral a part of her composition as a speaker pausing for breath. At times she abandoned her flamingo stance, straightened and stood erect, but only long enough to ease the strain on her back and legs.

As I quietly entered for a cup of coffee or a glass of water, I would linger, idly trolling about, gazing out the too-high oblong window at the pigeons preening their marbleized breasts on the roof of a terra-cotta building across the street, or putter about in a cramped cupboard for a toothpick, a tea bag, all the while watching her from the corner of my eye, seeing her studied profile only when her curtain of hair was tucked back. And then, as the gathering clouds turned the daylight through the kitchen window into a dull gray flannel, she would stop, her pencil perpendicular above the page like a stylus ready to descend; her one facing eye would narrow and a fine venation of wrinkles would sprout from its corner; her lips would thin into a prim smile, and that electrical surge, that rolling, blustery farrago of thought, that seismic dervish would froth up inside me, scramble the more mundane functions my brain was trying to execute, and hold me in its mute, starkly mute and wrathful eye until slowly Maria slipped back, brought her pencil in contact with the page and resumed writing. Quaking, sometimes without that object that had attracted me to the kitchen in the first place, I would return to my desk and take deep, febrile breaths.

I was satisfied that Maria's complex patterns and symphonic thoughts, and my proximity to her creative processes, were the sources of my destructive silences. But why, I would wonder, was I still prey to the same psychic interferences even during her brief absences, when I believed she was safely out of range? When she would be gone for an hour or more to the market to pick up some bok choy or baby carrots, I would hurry to my desk and sink back into my work, only to encounter the same scyllan havoc and charybdisian whorls. That Maria, wherever she was, was lapsing into similar concentrations at the same moment was highly unlikely. I suffered from the encroaching shadow of a memory; I was a mouse pressing the button and still rippling with the enervative shock though the current had been disconnected. What I had tried to do before we were such constant companions—conjure up her probing eye, keep her mystical presence always within my circadian sphere—was now an irreducible item of my existence.

At the time, however, that was the beauty of my chosen situation; that was the hindering, but nevertheless proud, color of love. Her penetration and ubiquitous presence in my life was like the crimson birthmark in Hawthorne's story, and to eradicate it would eradicate me. It upset and irritated me (in a practical sense, for I couldn't get anything done), but I believed the debilitation would pass; that the macule of irritation would be the core around which I would spin some silky, symmetrical pearl, the charm for which I would eventually forge a locket.

This occlusion was not strictly psychological, however. The air was full of her dust; my apartment was laden with Maria's tangible residue (of course, at that time I called it "our" apartment, but that was just a bit of quaint semantics, for it was, as she had told Violet, like every other place she'd ever lived— with the possible exception of the flat of her infancy—a *pied-à-terre*), much of it suspiciously located, strewn where I was sure to run into it. For as I worked in her absent periods, patiently, gingerly, trying to stay the swallowing and spewing of frenzied thought (when I began to detect these dark and ominous rumblings, I dropped my pen, rose and paced, thought about some trivial thing, took out the garbage, washed some dishes— something that Maria, despite her incessant dirtying of them, despised and blatantly avoided. On some later occasion, miffed over not finding one clean drinking glass and forced to take my water from a measuring cup, I reminded her of the now-late James Beard's statement that a good cook always cleans up after himself. She harrumphed and snarled "James Beard!" in a way I imagine Nietzsche might respond if someone mentioned Wagner, then smiled deviously and scratched something down on an index card), I would stop in midsentence, the thought complete but unwritten, so that I might ease right back into my work when I returned to my desk. Going into the bathroom, the phrase still dangling from the edge of my brain like a long filigrane of spittle, I would unexpectedly run across some *in petto* Maria: a teardrop cotton ball with traces of mascara, exuding the sweet peach fragrance of her scented cold cream; an intricately woven doily of raven hair that had settled atop the bathtub trap; a sanguine daub of tooth gel that had dripped and gone unnoticed, stiffened on the ridge of the scalloped bowl; the tongue depressor-shaped, nearly opaque, shiny paper backing to a feminine product, balanced on the rim of the wastebasket like the lost feather of some passing bird. These were not just bits of careless fluff that confirmed the presence of another person; these were the lilting, lyrical themes and recapitulating melodies of a grand, intoxicating composition, one mellifluous phrase melding into another, and another, until the whole work, with contrasting solos, spirited refrains, and reverent largos, was resonating through the chambers of my suddenly acoustical brain. And my thought, the minor nursery rhyme I had brought along for safekeeping, had fled amidst the glorious hubbub.

Meanwhile, back at the range, spinach was in the air. Banded bunches, their firm, soiled roots blushed pink, crammed our vegetable bin; piles of large, spatulate potherb brimmed over the top of a colander; the crimped, incised leaves formed a wilting head on many a grocery sack; its rich, loamy smell greeted me from the lethal cavity of the garbage disposal. Maria plunged handfuls of it into bubbling pots of water or broth, pureed it with oils and spices and other vegetables, made it the raw, flouncy bed for various entrées.

Some of our best works are those that spring from playfulness: a half-serious divertissement between the projects we deem of greater importance, like tossed-out observations we make snidely under our breath. It is only when we step back and examine things in a more objective light, if such a thing is possible, that we see the superior quality and unpretentious clarity of that which we doodled while talking on the telephone. Undertakings which we speak of somberly with determined faces, and grapple with as if they are death itself come a'calling, usually turn out to be silly, unreadable things.

The pages accumulated, the index cards piled up, but as far as Maria was concerned, she was simply dallying with a pleasing, but relatively insignificant, aspect of a more important whole. Her spinach notes multiplied. But why, and for how long, and to what end? As so often happens, half of the headwork and notework to *Spinacea oleracea* was complete before she realized that the project existed.

It was an August evening of high humidity and little moon. What shone—tiny, buffed with flour—disappeared for long periods behind banks of clouds, then showed its blurred, thumbnail face to me over a hill, or around the corner of a dark building as I walked home from working late on the wharf. Shrimp clung to me. I recall my feelings as I approached my building: of unexpectedly being invigorated despite the fatiguing day, of the alternating crabbing chills and rushes of warmth, of the sudden desire to get inside my apartment. A crush of unspecific thoughts were running through my head, thoughts that signaled by their very presence a certain clearness of mind and alerted me, it seemed, that I might accomplish something if I could just get to my desk and begin to sort them out.

This is very difficult for me to describe, but from time to time, I am suffused with these feelings, as if my mind has fortuitously clicked into a mode that lends itself to writing, where my thoughts are not just jumbled, errant impulses, but have attached themselves to real words or phrases, and are bumping and ricocheting around in search of a sentence. This is the ideal state, the one we constantly try to achieve and maintain, and though we can sometimes artificially provoke it, it usually shows up when we are in the shower or, as I was, walking home. This was what welled up inside me as I entered my apartment building and bounded up the steps. The hot corridor smelled of moist paint, sweat and rotting plants. My doorknob was sticky. A grocery cart with one wobbling wheel nosed out of the apartment two doors down, then clatteringly withdrew when the young Asian lad pushing it realized I had seen him (this fellow enjoyed stealing and collecting carts, and one of the tenants had reported him to our landlord, Mr. Diagiacomo, who warned him not to bring any more into the building). From somewhere came the nasal, urgent voices of a television drama, complete with popping pistols and squealing tires.

I finally found my key and pushed open the door. The room was smotheringly hot. The air smelled of spearmint and lemon grass. Scratching madly in her notebook was Maria, in a lotus position on the Murphy bed, the flimsy muslin sheets disheveled and bunched around her like an immense hemicycle of meringue. She was wearing a white tank top, and a Rorschach of perspiration (a hypodermic needle) spread over her back. Though I created quite a breeze, she didn't notice my return, but the curtains at least greeted me, billowing full and fluttering a hello. It was a full five minutes, during which time I threw my fishy apron in the corner, pealed off my shirt, kicked off my shoes, and returned from the kitchen taking deep drinks from a water bottle, before she realized that I was home. It might have been much longer had she not just come to the end of her written tirade. My imagined eloquence, so vivid a moment before, had begun to melt when I entered that stifling room, and was gone with Maria's concluding pencil slash.

On that brutal summer evening, *Spinacea oleracea* opened its sensitive little eyes after its silent, secret period of incubation. What she had written was the first of several proposed introductions to the work. Many more would be bandied about in the remaining days of composition, some with long passages excised and rewritten, others that just varied slightly from one another, and one or two that were wildly different from the entire lot and from the one eventually chosen for publication. But in the end she came nearly full circle, and her final preface is closest, contentwise at least, to that very first draft. It sits before me now, one of the few manuscript pieces that she mislaid and neglected to take with her. The page is rumpled and mottled from moisture; the purple dye of the rules has bled in some spots. Her penciled scrawl is ashen, faded to translucence by age. My regular handling of it will soon dissolve her words for all time. Though the strange, atypical drafts might be more interesting to those who have read her book, it is the original one that smacks most of the inspired, unbridled Maria, the girl behind the hazy mesh of her tulle veil, the perspiring artist. Even with our rudimentary knowledge of her origins and influences, this early piece—which was eventually cooled and skimmed—is revelatory. More than just a diatribe on a vegetable, it will give the attentive reader a keen view of the intricate shadings of her complex character. My heart aches as I quote it at length:

     . . . it is the elusive vegetable, mysterious and obscure

because of the very indifference it elicits. It is a chameleon of essences, not changing its color except under considerable contrivance—in fact, its deep emerald shade is the only thing with which it is comfortable—but only its shape and texture. Of these there are, for all intents and purposes, two: raw and cooked. Not much variation there. And it is so unsure of itself that these are diametrically opposed. It is the hue of its flavor and the importance of its presence that fade and flourish. It is amenable to nearly every dish and manner of cooking, maddeningly unassuming; by its very nature, it is meek and subordinate. It much prefers to assimilate itself or simply, unobtrusively embellish something or other. It changes eagerly and willingly, and unlike many other vegetables or spices, does not need to be precisely calculated or put through procrustean paces to achieve the desired state, the desired flavor. It shirks and shrinks from the limelight. Indeed, when it sits alone on the edge of a plate, it appears weepy and ashamed and will, despite the most strenuous strainings and drainings, invariably leak its weak green moisture toward the other portions in a pitiful attempt to blend in. Even when at the peak of its flavor, it is terribly self-conscious and will give itself over to the tiniest trickle of butter or the lightest dusting of pepper. It wants to be anything but itself . . .

. . . if one composes a list of the foods most often despised by children, spinach is likely to turn up (right before turnips), though curiously spinach should not bear the blame for its unpopularity. Unlike liver or beets or brussels sprouts or sauerkraut, reviled for their exoticism and radically divergent tastes, thus giving them the distinction of being called 'acquired' (in much the same way that we acquire a taste for a particular work or specific style of painting that, in our innocent, naive youth, made absolutely no sense to us), spinach falls clearly within the realm of a generally palatable and moderately colored edible. There is nothing unsettling or strange about it. . . and, like the hero who ate lightning and crapped thunder, Popeye ate spinach and pummeled brutes and bullies. He protected his weaker friends and always did the right thing, thanks to a good dose of the greens. Why, then, is spinach so abhorred? Its poor posture? Its kelplike demeanor? Perhaps spinach reminds children of spooky Spanish moss that hangs from trees in the wildly overgrown yard of a vacant, groaning old manse down the street? Or the reeking, dripping seaweed that squishes and trails the creature that extricates itself from the ocean floor and stalks their soft dreams? Where does it get its crummy reputation?

Surely its name contributes to the shoddy treatment it gets. Two hard syllables form a bark of reproach, and putting an "Achtung!" before it gives one a command of sharp, edgy symmetry. It is nothing like the round, maternal "corn" or the gay, smiley "peas." "Spinach" is a dire imperative and for some children no doubt constitutes a challenge . . .

. . . it is the rich and fertile standout in eggs Florentine; it is the delicate and essential network to the Quiche Lorraine; mixed with feta and wrapped in an evanescent strudel, it has a subtle, slippery and intoxicating flavor that is practically blissful. . .

The pertinent published passages are mere echoes of these plangent excerpts. Only in the moments when she was speaking specifically of herself (recall some earlier bits of quoted text), and these are decidedly rare, did she allow a certain depth of feeling to impose itself on the subject. Emotions and easily identified snatches of personality were otherwise banished. She was tightfisted and frugal with the most subjective of her feelings, and much of her insight is carefully detached.

The day *Spinacea oleracea* officially began is separate and distinct, and is of greater importance than even the day we met or the day she moved in with me. Not necessarily because it is of "literary significance," as raconteurs and anecdotists might label it, nor because it was the instance that produced my most cherished piece of Maria Perpetua memorabilia. No, it was on that dogged, sticky day, as I drank cool water and watched Maria disentangle her cashew legs and fall back on the bed, her chest dewy with sweat, a few black colubrine hairs clinging to her neck and throat, that I realized my efforts of the last several weeks had been but vain, anfractuous undertakings, and that the only way to remedy this was to make Maria's current work, whatever it was, my first and only order of creative business. I did not pause to entertain what the long-term consequences of this might be. They were irrelevant. Just as, in regards to my relationship with Maria, I could not make out the figures and their doings in the distance, so it was with myself, now gripped in her pythonine presence. I suppose the casual observer might consider this a rash, knee-jerking response: that I was frail and weak; that I quailed at the slightest bit of confounding discontent; that I should have faced my vast and terrible silence like a man, like a poet-warrior; that I should have raged against it to the very ends of my frayed and hemorrhaging ability. In every man's life there are things he should do, but doesn't.

Beyond that, I am inclined to remain deadly silent, but of course I can't. My creativeness was rent; my self-perception was in ruins. If, in trying to explain myself, we inch our examination light a bit closer to the authoress, then it will be useful.

I contemplate the nature of genius. I try to understand it, though greater, more analytical minds than mine make such investigation their inconclusive life's work. It is so complex and unfathomable that the only thing we know about it is it constantly defies any framework or rigid set of traits we try to impose on it. As soon as we say, "Geniuses are notoriously contemptuous of organized religions," we run across a brilliant fellow who embraces Catholicism as heartily as the pontiff. Or if we say, "Whatever a genius does or creates, he does because he is compelled to do it," the hailed artist, the consummate composer falls silent and disappears into the well of obscurity. One may say that this is because he was too intelligent for this world, that the absurdity of it all dawned on him, but I tend to think that one needn't be a genius to recognize the absurdity of existence. Lesser men succumb to absurdity: the genius vaults it, continues in spite of it.

But I do believe that the genius, whatever his field, recognizes something that others do not: the incalculable importance of his work. He may appear to those of us who cannot comprehend the magnitude of what he does to be a fine mind frittering away on the fringe. But the genius realizes that his work is vital, vital in a shared way. The activity is predicated on his existence, and his existence is predicated on the activity.

Not only is his art sustained, and sustaining, not only is he inseparable from it by necessity, like a man with a mechanical heart, but he gets an inimitable pleasure from it. He is a Sisyphus, but a thoroughly happy, joyous Sisyphus, whistling gaily, cuffing up his sleeves and putting his shoulder to the stone.

I do not mull this over because I am trying to present Maria as a genius now, or because I considered her to be a genius then. I merely say it because she did display that geniuslike quality, and it had an inarguably profound effect on me. One may say, "If we are to accept this as a criterion for geniuslike, then the successful businessman, the pastry chef, the coal miner, the typographer and the pop musician are *potential* geniuses." I agree. They are potential geniuses. The reader now balks, understandably, believing that I devalue the word "genius" by applying it so broadly. Though that may be so, I believe that at the same time I *enhance* the value of the human being. And that is not such a bad result in a world where there are so few True Genuises, Realized Geniuses. For why should the gifted educator be any less appreciated and respected than the gifted concert violinist? We are all potential geniuses in a way. We fall short through no fault or laziness of our own because our intellect is just not of that chimerical, superior quality necessary to propel us into the loftiest and most rarefied level of Realized Genius. The Realized Genius is not just in the vanguard: he is beyond the vanguard. He is not alone at the top of the heap; he hovers above that fleshy tangle of limbs. For all our commendable achievements, crowded trophy cases, and folders bulging with kudos, we are still earthbound, valiantly stretching our fingers toward the stars, while the Realized Genius is already there, cavorting with constellations and hobnobbing with nebulae.

As I stood there mechanically gulping and bloating myself on water (no longer from thirst, but because I was so lost in my musings that I forgot to tell myself to stop drinking), I speculated on the possibility that we were both enmeshed in something quite extraordinary and monumental, with Maria at the controls and me tinkering with the astrolabe, making certain that we stayed on course. My choices did not seem very difficult, and thanks to the last several weeks of my stutterings and false starts, the sacrifice did not appear all that great, did not, in fact, appear to be a sacrifice at all, but a strange opportunity, spherical and golden. And let us not forget the other soliciting circumstances. I can list them, but I cannot convey their alogical importance: I was in love with her; I marveled at her undefined ability, her very existence; I reveled in the convoluted immensity of her and feared her at the same time, the way one who celebrates Nature also fears her incredible capacity for destruction. Such were my timorous justifications, my poor reasons for choosing silent subservience over artistic struggle with all its pits and boils. It seems so obviously erroneous now, and yet . . .

I looked at her inverted face. Her eyes rolled and pitched beneath their pale mauve lids as if she were in a crowded, hectic dream. Then, amused by a thought of her own, or perhaps sensing I was watching her, her mouth curled into a smile that looked—from my upside-down view of her, her small chin in the approximate position of a nose—like the peculiar, animated frown of an eyeless hand puppet. I crouched at the foot of the bed and ran a cool hand up her leg, kissed along her calf that was nubbled with dark pinpoints, lingered at the dank, lamb-scented crook of her knee, and paused at its ovate cap which bore, from some girlhood tumble, a vermicular, sgraffito scar about a centimeter long and white as marshmallow.

That evening—like a sovereign hoping to appease the clamorous malcontents and critics of his regime—I relinquished partial control of my desk, cleared scraps and sundries, redistributing them through the first and third drawers and leaving the shallow second and cavernous fourth for Maria to use as she wished. Not a paper clip, eraser or rubber band did I leave behind, as some are in the habit of doing when emptying drawers and cabinets and running across homeless, minuscule morsels that have sunk to the bottom and now have no logical receptacle, no place to go, and are of little or no value. (These things are usually toothpicks that have escaped their box, or bottle caps that were once saved for some arcane reason, but different people leave different things, and I have moved into apartments that still held the prior occupant's screwdrivers, clay flowerpots, cleaning supplies and, one time, a medieval-looking piece of sadomasochistic headgear that I could not quite figure out.) I even went so far as to scrape up a three-year-old Easter Seal—a tiny stamp upon which a blazing menorah was displayed next to the organization's patriarchal cross—that had tenaciously adhered itself to the wood.

That minor exodus completed, I informed Maria of the vacancy rather nonchalantly (though, for my own peculiar reasons, I ached for her to occupy the space), and for the duration of her tenure, never opened those modest storage areas again. Even for several sorrowful weeks after she had left, I could not bring myself to look into them, as if fearing the detonation of some smoky, sentimental bomb disguised as an innocent fragment—a scribbled note, a hairpin, a dusting of eraser excelsior, some leaden ash from her cigarette—but when I finally summoned the courage, I found them as whistle-clean as the day they had been emptied. Perhaps she had never bothered to use them. So they remained until I began the note gathering and composition of this very manuscript, which has found solace and dreamless sleep therein for the few hours when I am not pouring over these painful pages. The dark, anechoic cherrywood confines are a worthy and apropos receptacle.

SEVEN

Much of this chronicle has been intriguing, illuminating and, of all things, easy. Before I began its actual writing, I feared that my melancholic pangs and pinings would be quagmire, and my spinning wheels would only immure me more deeply in my debilitating silence. But much of it has been palliative and painless. The introspection that is intrinsic to retrospection has helped me unravel many misunderstood, involute threads that have long lain in a ridiculous, mangled heap. Glancing back at the introductory pages I wrote a few weeks ago, I detect a tang of reproach. The fingers that clacked out the beginning of this story were rude, accusatory ones, and indeed my recollections began as more of an indictment. But as the evidence was tagged, and the witnesses called, those fingers retracted, that rhetoric softened.

At the outset, when I imagined Maria reading this, I saw her livid and fuming, feeling betrayed and violated. Now I see her, wherever she is (the fashionable columns and members of the culturati say you are in New York, ma amie, or thereabouts; is it really true? Sometimes I get the ticklish, ironic notion that you are back in Pennsylvania), as more patient and even wistful: still disapproving, but with a far-gentler and sisterly disapproval, shaking her head with a bemused smile and affecting an avuncular "tsk, tsk" from time to time. It is not the content I see her finding unacceptable, but my impassioned, contrite style. For I know, Maria, that your finely tailored work would never be tinted and tainted with such psychological musings and emotional meanderings. The plinking of such personal heartstrings has no place in Art, and I surrender that point to you. I will not attempt to argue it here, for I humbly admit (and this should certainly give you reason to smile, if nothing has up until now) that this is not Art, but a step toward it, a preface to art, a passage to artistic recrudescence. I have been circumambulating the person I once was, or the person I shall be, spiraling slowly in, following a cochleate path that is inching me ever closer, ever closer . . .

And as I said, it has been a far-smoother journey than I had envisioned. Only when I approach some spinach, when those great green leaves rise up before me, do I balk, recoil, backpedal, and stumble over the depressed ridges of my footsteps. I despise it, view it as the internecine interloper, though I know that if it hadn't been spinach, it would have been something else.

Radishes, or endive. Still that does not calm my anxiety. In the market I inevitably run across it, though I try to look the other way and hurry by. But it always stops me, beckons to me, tempts me with the memories it holds, stings me with its implications. I see it, richly green and ruffled, piled thickly on its inclined display and sparkling with droplets of moisture from the produce man's spray gun, or crammed into cellophane bags and stacked, a bed of tiny emerald throw pillows. One day, a very very short time ago, I even considered buying some and preparing it, thinking that by facing it, by coming to terms with it, I could surmount it, finish this memoir swiftly and surely, and be done with all of it. I was close, Maria, so close: I held a bunch in my cold fingers; I shook off some of its globular beads; I felt confident, hopeful, holding it over my basket, when suddenly a fat, hideous, brown beetlelike bug pushed its way through the thicket of stems and scurried across my Mount of Mars. I screamed, terrified, convulsed, and flung it across the aisle, where it landed, roots up, like a bright, gaudy wig, atop a casaba melon. And I rushed from the store, a booming, big-eminy pulse pounding in my temples.

That harried episode strikes me as quite metaphorical. For, at this point in our story, the beetle that is Maria keeps scampering out from my remembered verdure and startling me. She is hidden amidst all that dark vegetation, and each time I try to understand it by itself, she pops up to confuse the issue. Conversely, when I try to see things solely in terms of Maria, or Maria and I—two human beings wholly separate from cooking and art—spinach sprouts up through the cracks in the pavement. From that point onward, the greens and the girl, the spinach and the siren, are inseparable.

Our relationship had begun its inexorable decline, yet I can offer no demonstrative evidence to support this. It must suffice to say that the closer her book came to completion, the closer our affair came to dissolution. Everything contributed to her work, everything had a purpose, and her work also touched everything else. So when it was finished, when the idea had come to fruition and its abstractions vanished, so did the importance of its incidental influences. That spinach and I occupied equal space in her life was mere coincidence. If I had come into the picture afterward, I am sure that I would have lasted only as long as her next endeavor. But she did not consciously structure things in this way; it was not her plan to acquire and discard as it suited her. That was just the way things turned out. Reflexes of self-preservation.

The surface of our lives offered no clues to the gradual dissipation of our relationship, and even now, as I strain to recall the events and activities of those days, nothing protrudes: everything is as slick and gleaming as glass. I continued at the seafood bar through the balmy days of autumn amidst bicycles and brightly clad tourists, through another fine season, another eternity of blue sky. The wharf was a venue I seemed to have played forever, and I arrived there each morning for another rote performance with the usual assemblage of tireless characters, with the addition of an occasional ingenue here, an understudy there: the stooped, bewhiskered friend several paces away who, for a nominal fee, stamped one's penny with a cable car or an easily recognizable bridge; the comrade on the opposite corner, the Human Jukebox, who sat hidden in his hut of varicolored, tessellated curtains and brilliant pastel signs, keeping his eye on his customers and onlookers through a clever arrangement of mirrors (it occurs to me that ever after my countless days around the wharf, I have never caught a glimpse of this curious fellow).

And yet, despite the constantly swimming multitude of impossibly similar faces, despite the mechanical sameness of my duties (pass crab, pass shrimp, pass bread, take money, make change, fill cups, replenish ice, pass crab . . .), this work was, for the first time, different, utterly different, for it was not done solely to maintain my existence and my existence alone, but to buttress and benefit the existence of someone else. I was a patron, philanthropist, sponsor, housemother, cheerleader, coaxer, wheedler, coddler, editor, comforter. My work, my life, had a strange, hypnotic, inevitable quality. The monied masses poured in and out; the sun rose and set; the boats bobbed on the bay; a flaxen-haired girl in a white jumper and painter's cap set up each morning across the street—a new player—and put her breath to a sweet, silvered flute that came alive with jigs and bagatelles, the sun bursting in asterisms off its wavering shaft. Life's tiny events transpired, halcyon time flowed; somewhere, someone might very likely have been flipping through the back issue of some obscure quarterly and stopped to prod a hibernating poem of mine while at the same time, in an unremarkable apartment with cream-colored walls a few dozen blocks away, Maria Perpetua pressed her indicia into some formerly forgettable and theretofore mundane spinach dish.

How slavish was my servitude? What heights altruism? I flinch at these words, for their hum is discordant and negative, yet any others that might enhance the positive would obfuscate the accuracy. Dedication? An understatement. Commitment? Too weak and nebulous. I simply acted in a way that I felt would be most appropriate, most prudent to the work at hand. She wrote, she cooked, and I—lap perpetually blanketed with a napkin—ingested concoction after spinach concoction, resolved to maintain a discerning eye and an objective palate. I banished parochialism and predilections—not that I had so many—and kept an open mind and mouth. I surprised myself.

One October evening I hustled home just as the sun was nearly set, and the sky glowing beyond the buildings was pink as lox. I was in a jaunty, convivial mood, anticipating a poetry reading at a nearby café, and hoping that Maria could not only spare my assistance that evening (I had warned her of potential plans when I left for work, but she was moon-eyeing her folios and taking pregnant draws on a cigarette, and it was impossible to tell if her affirmative grunts meant my words had been duly registered), but that she might also accompany me. When I returned, she was in the kitchen, cussing and muttering vulgar oaths, clumsily wielding a can opener, trying to shuck oysters. Categorically I find oysters the most odious comestible I have ever had the opportunity to eat. I cannot speak for such exotic oddities as goat's eyes or stuffed moose head (an unparalleled, squeal-provoking delicacy in Chinese households, when they can get it); I might very well find them equally repulsive should the occasion to eat them ever arise. But of the foods commonly consumed in this part of the world, even certain organ meats and other raw sea creatures do not garner the same disdain I feel for that slimy mollusk. It is not flavor that causes me to turn my head and bring my hand to my mouth, but the fact that oysters are best loved when they are the least dead. Something savored raw is one thing, but something that is at its peak and must be gobbled up while still alive is something else entirely. And, Maria being the fastidious stickler she was, I feared the worst. Even if I had been catatonic, I do not think I could have allowed those briny, membranous organisms to pass through my lips and slither down my throat, no matter what chaser she had provided. My heart sank. The poetry reading suddenly seemed like a mirage, a remote fantasy, like the thought of a prosperous, comfortable old age is to a man being led down the hall to the electric chair.

Standing stock-still and incredulous, I wanted to turn and flee. For the first and only time in our acquaintance, I was flushed with an urge to move away from her instead of toward her. Her elbow flapped up and down, her muscles tensed and relaxed, tensed and relaxed, the flesh of her upper arm quivered as she struggled to insert the blunt, hawk-nosed point of the opener into the shell's hinge. And for a brief, disquieting moment, I did not know who she was, who I was or what I was doing there, as if some jesting providence had swept me up and deposited me in another time, another place, just for a lark. Finally she turned and looked at me, one eye squinched shut, her lips pursed and pulled comically to one side, a fine sheen of perspiration in the hollow of her throat. She dropped her metal weapon onto the countertop with a *pling!* and waved her hand at me, beckoning.

"Hanky, hanky!"

I whipped one from my back pocket, quick as a prestidigitator, and handed it to her. "A bit of 'oyster liquor,'" she said and pressed it to her closed eye. "Seadog that you are, you wouldn't know how to pry these things open, would you? Is there some magic word one must utter?"

"The best oyster is a closed oyster," I muttered. "Maria, remember . . ."

"Well, I can't make Oysters Rockefeller with closed oysters, mon ami," she said, blotting the sweat on her neck. "Can I now?"

Then, holding the kerchief to her throat, she smiled at me patiently, expectantly. We shared a long, articulate pause, the dull hum of tense, terrible silence, and as her indulgent smile began to wilt, so did my resolve. I joined her at the kitchen counter. As she set about creaming her rich ingredients, I reduced our struggling friends to their doomed, half-shell state.

"Besides," she said gaily, triumphantly, dashing Tabasco, dashing Worcestershire, "you will enjoy these oysters."

"And just how can you be so sure?"

"Because *I* am making them," she said and kissed my hot ear. "The way to a man's stomach is through his heart."

And in a room blue with smoke and somber as an orthodox mass, a poet was reciting his own rhythmic impressions of life and love.

She gathered speed. She blazed by on ludicrously small amounts of sleep, swept up and hurtled along on the sheer momentum of her creative intensity. And it did not seem to take a physical toll on her. I would roll over in bed in midalertness, expecting to bump softly into her slight, warm body, only to flop into the void created by the absence of an accustomed partner, and would open my eyes to see Maria at the desk, her back as straight as an oak, writing, writing, as crisp and keen-eyed as if it were the middle of the day. The adrenaline of one who believes he has overslept would burst through me, and I would snap up like a shiv blade, fumbling with the binding bedclothes until I caught sight of the clock and realized that the light in the room was her desk lamp, and that dawn was still hours away. And that same evening I'd return, we would dine, converse, tumble through acts of love, and before any languor could take hold, she would be at her desk in her flannel tunic (she'd amputated the sleeves during a long-lost week of beastly humidity), composing once more, shuffling cards, contemplating the movements of some smooth, adroit apparition that was dancing about the studio, visible to her alone. Every so often she would lay her pencil aside and rest her locked hands atop her head, as if to keep the top of her skull from popping off. Her lyrate, slender limbs were milk white in the blanching fluorescence, and beneath each armpit was a shaded, pruinose oval of polleny deodorant.

I remained awake, usually reading, sipping coffee or chamomile tea, hoping to last until she extinguished the light and climbed into bed, but she never seemed to flag, and soon my eyelids began to flutter and my head wobbled like a faltering top. She always outlasted me. Sometimes she left her desk to usher me to bed, pulled the contraption out of the wall, and planted a quick, dry kiss right between my rheumy eyes. But I began falling asleep in my reading chair so regularly, staunchly refusing to go to bed until the specter of sleep had firmly taken hold of my body, that she just let me snooze wherever and in whatever position I happened to assume until she was ready to retire for a few, light, diaphanous hours. Groggily pummeling my pillow, on the verge of slipping back into the nothingness, I watched her emerge from the bathroom, move around the bed, and as she peeled off whatever she wore, her body in the charged darkness was enveloped by a web of crackling, blue static.

When she wasn't working at home, she spent hours in the library. This was most often in the afternoon while I worked, but occasionally in the early evening, the need for a certain bit of information, a clarification of some historical canard she'd gleaned the day before, an etymology, presented itself, and the resolution of this suspicious contradiction or the excavation of that obscure curio grew to such proportions that she could not leave it until the next day. And off she went, a litter of pads and papers under her arm, a taxi-colored pencil distressed with teethmarks tucked in the crook of her invisible ear.

One night near Christmas, the only Christmas we spent together, she abruptly jumped up from her desk as if someone had shouted "Fire!" hastily gathered papers, collected various books that were lying about, and pulled on a pair of jeans, readying herself to take off for her third flight to the library that day. I was silent, but my resigned, slack face oozed disappointment. She pulled on a blazer of mine, the nearest wrap she could find (so spacious that her hands never emerged from the sleeves) and was at the door when she caught sight of my pouty demeanor. Setting her things aside, she perched on my lap, pushed her sleeves above her elbows, folded her slim arms around my neck and drew my head to her chest. Beneath the thick folds of fabric, the prickly brush of tweed, she smelled of vanilla with a faint pentimento of talcum. Somewhere Handelian orisons were playing. She nested a silent kiss on the top of my head and whispered promises to me—child that I was—of thick, frothy eggnog and dimly lit intimacies when she returned.

Her enchanting assurances calmed me, but a few hours later when she still hadn't returned, I was sick with fear that she had been accosted, abducted, murdered. The library had been closed for nearly two hours. I retraced her usual route, looking for telltale pages, books dropped in a scuffle. I plumbed the black coulisses between buildings, the alleys where capricious light distorted shapes and cast denatured shadows. Crumpled bodies turned to bags of garbage by the time I reached them. Fleeing rapists were merely phantasms conjured by light and wind, playing tricks in the periphery of my vision. At the end of my nervous, peregrine path was the library, hopelessly dark and sealed tight. Fear turned to grief. I plopped down on the steps; a bladder of sobs expanded in my throat, ready to burst. Kneading my forehead, racked with indecision, I was on the verge of rechecking the area more thoroughly (if such a thing were possible), trying to convince myself that there was a plausible explanation, that while I had been perusing rubbish, she had slipped by me and was probably already home folding eggs and cream, thinking I had popped off to the store. Then, from the library entrance came the clinking of turning locks, along with a throaty, disgruntled voice, and as the door was wrenched open, out flew Maria, a disorganized ream of papers clasped to her chest, one or two of them fluttering off behind her—like feathers from a wounded, plummeting goose—as she skipped down the steps. The door boomed soundly shut. In a corner recess at some desk carrel, behind a battlement of dusty books, Maria had fallen asleep unnoticed. She was still sleeping ("drooling on a Funk and Wagnall's") when a janitor blundered upon her and shooed her out.

"I was sitting there, wide awake," she said as we walked home, "writing, and then I stopped. I was in the middle of all that silence and gold light, and that close fustiness from all those old texts, and it was very peaceful, and I fell into such a meditation that I didn't feel quite alive. Or no, no, I didn't feel like a person—that's what it was, just a very dense, benevolent consciousness floating there, and those books were like a form of consciousness also, and then . . ." she trailed off and shook her head.

"Then what?" I asked, shifting the bundle of her materials from one arm to another.

She shuddered and clung closely to my arm, unwilling to elucidate further. In the startled confusion and alacrity of her departure, she'd left my blazer draped over the back of the library chair.

The year rolled over and died, but I doubt if she noticed it. She kept firmly, unwaveringly on without missing a beat, as if all the past days were but one, and a long sleepless night was still stretched out ahead of us. That winter was dull, full of rain and mist; my hours were cut back and I had many free days. On the Saturday morning I was aroused by whistling gales and lentil-sized hailstones that skittered across our windows like a handful of tossed pebbles, Maria announced that the time had come to begin transcribing some of her early handwritten sections to typescript, and since she could not work a typewriter with any amount of competence, the task fell to me.

I wound a sheet of good strong bond around the platen of my Underwood and was ready to go. That first day was frightfully unproductive. She had decided to begin the introduction, but as there were several versions, many repetitive, none definitive, she spent the bulk of our morning session with scissors and glue, cutting apart paragraphs from this or that draft and pasting them to a piece of cardboard in their supposed order, peeling them up and rearranging them, or striking them out completely, superimposing new atop old, then realizing that the paragraph she'd buried was the one she had originally intended to retain. After she had dissected and hopelessly jumbled two or three versions, she abandoned the cardboard reconstruction and began rewriting snippets in longhand on her note cards, giving each a number and passing them to me. Her constant, vacillating revisions were a nuisance; I would type for a minute or two, sit for five, type for another minute, and then she would request all the cards to be handed back to her so that she might renumber them, and I would have to start again. After some considerable efforts, we finally managed to get one complete typewritten page. I made the mistake of triumphantly announcing this, at which point she demanded to see it for herself (as if such panther-quick progress were not to be believed), and after reading it over quickly, she began to snort and stutter, checking her temper (not too effectively), saying that the arrangement was wrong, all wrong, and that *I* had transposed several cards. I produced the cards in their supposed order—by now they had three or four numbers scrawled across the top, which were crossed out, renumbered, or had old numbers recircled or thickly outlined to reestablish their place—and after shuffling through them, exasperated and annoyed, she expelled a great lungful of smoke that hung in a cloud above her head, and made the welcome suggestion that we break for lunch.

A *mauvais quart d'heure*, that lunch, as I recall. I sipped Earl Grey and munched Maria's spinach tea sandwiches while she merely stroked her forehead and smoked, staring off into another part of the room, formulating her next move. Our lack of conversation was unsettling, a great vow of silence that I dared not breach, and my chewing of those countless, crustless triangles, my egregious slurps of hot tea, would have been terribly obstreperous had they not been muffled by a persistent wind and the susurrous passing of occasional autos. When she'd finally decided, perhaps, that I'd had enough to eat, she tossed her head, brushed some ashes from her lap and stood up from the table. The introduction, she said, would be the last thing to complete. We would concentrate on the chapters. Only when the book was finished, and we were residing in its cool, demulcent shadow, would she write her preface.

Had I found the courage to speak during that lunch, I would have suggested that very plan, as it seemed to be the most logical and expedient course of action. The final third of her book was yet unwritten, much composition and many ideas lay ahead, ideas that were still nonexistent in the curving scope of her vision and would not appear for several weeks. As new material was composed, old material was summarily run once more through the alembic of her overall conception. Her introduction, if she'd decided to write it first, would no doubt have been wheeled back into surgery at the close of each day.

So I began transforming her writhing lines of rumination and recipes into pellucid, uniform stripes of type. Her handwriting was an especial oddity, for it would begin a subtle metamorphosis in the midst of a sentence until, a few lines later, it was completely different. A page would begin with a small, compact, right-leaning script of tiny serifs and modest descenders and slowly evolve into an upright creature. After tramping along like this for a leisurely sentence or two, it would start its obtuse tilt, as if her words were bending over backward to get their point across. Then, as if this style were suddenly unendurable (it was certainly a torment to the eye, this catenulate line of letters, nearly prone as if being blown by the mighty sirocco of inspiration), it would snap erect once more, this time assuming a semicursive, semiprinted appearance. This was far more legible, but replete with many more quirks. Her lowercase "a" was a self-conscious little thing that could not decide which form it preferred. On first appearance it was of the pointed-head, small-cap variety, next it was a tiny, one-celled organism with the hint of a tail, and finally it affected the pretentious manner of roman type, its ample potbelly resting languidly on the mauve line.

This is just a smattering of the idiosyncrasies, for there were innumerable variations, overlaps, and triple, quadruple mergings. Every so often an aberration would crop up and just as quickly die, a unique flowery specimen that blossomed once and was seen no more. On a few occasions, typing steadily, I would be stopped dead in my clacks by a paragraph that could have been penned by me: a sentence that deftly mimicked my own hand's bisected "z," or the ligated sixteenth note of my double "f."

Far more fascinating, however, than her chameleon hand was an arcane, indecipherable charactery she had spontaneously developed in the course of her composition. Somewhere around Chapter 2 ("Emerald Cities"), I ran across a page where the words suddenly stopped and a mess of symbols that I mistook for doodles ensued. As I searched for the start of the next sentence, I finally realized that these shapes and squiggles represented something. A star, a cube, an arrow, a helix: only intermittently separated by an article, preposition or punctuation, and none of them ever recurring. When I asked her how I was supposed to type these things she snatched the page away from me, scrutinized it, her tongue tip peeking out from between her teeth, and began to dictate from the point I'd halted. Her words were fluid, measured, precise and pure as written English. While she was writing, it seemed that from time to time her thoughts had begun churning and whorling with such ferocity that a description, account, impression or phrase-turning sometimes evaporated while she was in the act of verbalizing its antecedent. In order to preserve as many of these bursts in their proper order as she could, she affixed them with a singular, evocative symbol and moved on. Amazingly these symbols represented not just words or short phrases, but sometimes entire passages that she'd squirreled away in her limber mind. A three-dimensional cube, a cluster of spheres, were the keys that unlocked these thoughts and brought them forth once more. She never explained this technique, most likely because she couldn't, but even if she had, it would probably have exceeded the limits of my comprehension.

As we plunged more deeply into the manuscript, the symbols became more frequent, the weather more temperate, the rain desisted by delicate degrees, and Maria—that bright, burning star at the center of our fragile universe—turned her beguiling, inquiring, swarthy eyes further inward. She was arcing toward the book's conclusion, producing new and primping old material by day, dictating to me by night. Returning from work late one afternoon, I noticed that the patiently growing stack of typed pages was gone. Maria was in the kitchen grating an immense, pungent wedge of Romano cheese.

"What's wrong?" I asked.

"Where?"

"Your manuscript?"

"O." She flipped the wedge and began grating the other side. "It's under consideration, I presume."

"By who?"

"By *whom*, mon ami. Significant others," she said, and though her back was still toward me, her face was mirrored in the bulbous bowl of the soup ladle hanging before her on the wall. I could not ascertain, however, if that image's Gioconda grin was a true reflection, or just the grotesque, fun-house effect of the rounded steel.

She was making her spinach pesto, a creamy pasta companion of fresh spinach, olive oil, garlic, cheese, parsley, pignolis and white pepper. As we did not have any machine that miraculously rendered noodles from the simple input of ingredients, Maria made her noodles by hand, one of the few bits of culinary custom she had gleaned from her grandmother and deemed worth remembering. Into a volcano of semolina she dropped her eggs and began paring down the inner sides of the crater with a fork, occasionally adding trickles of water when the dough became too glutinous and unmanageable. Once the dough had reached the proper consistency, she spread it flat along the countertop, dusted it a bit with more flour and rolled it. She would then slice off slender spirals, shake out the noodles, and spread them on a sheet of waxed paper until she was ready to drop them into a pot of boiling water.

The pesto, a garlicky, damp mulch, had a kind of rich, grassy flavor, an earthy aftertaste once the spices and the cheese melted away, but Maria showed neither pleasure nor contempt for the end result. As she sipped a glass of resiny Chianti (which had been opened more than a week before and bordered on vinegary insolence) and mopped softened noodles around her plate, there was a mutual disinterest between her and her food. My generous lip smacking and intentional, little tussive noises did not penetrate her vague, insentient reverie. Only when I mentioned that evening's dictation did she speak.

"My brain's not in it tonight," she said. "Let's go somewhere and have a drink."

The night was clear and navy blue and delightfully warm for a change. There is something about one of spring's first balmy evenings that begets a sense of comfortable community. The strangers on the street are no longer grim and tightly wrapped, bracing against some wind, some chill, but are airy, talkative, animated. Shops prop open their doors to the genial atmosphere, and share with the passerby their felicitous chatter; the beeps and jingles of a cash register; the smell of sizzling deep fat, of dense, beer-scented smoke, of perfume; the humming music of a jukebox. Yes, music is what I best recall, music is the order of such days. Music: reedy music from open car windows, music from the box on a young man's shoulder, live music from somewhere unknown, coming from a distance, thin, exhausted and porous as tissue by the time it reached us.

We hopped a bus to Coit Tower; there was music from the cars parked along the coiling drive. Girls sat on the stone parapet and looked over the city, occasionally raising an urgent voice to be heard above all the music. The luminous meadow of city lights reflected off the dome of the sky and formed a glowing layer as yellow as egg custard above the bumpy vista of hills and buildings. I swiveled the observation binoculars, shaped like a hooded cobra, and produced a quarter from behind her ear (an old trick I'd forgotten, until that time, to show her), and asked Maria if she wanted to look. She demurred with a grateful smile and slipped her fingers up to the second knuckle into the front pockets of her jeans, holding her shoulders in a shrug.

"Everything is so depthless at night," she said, "and besides, why do people go out of their way to get a panoramic view and then pay money to reduce it to the constricted field of a lens?"

"Why indeed," I said and returned the coin to its nook. Lingering there, I traced a fingertip along the nautilus-shaped ridge of her ear. "Coffee?" I asked.

"Yes. Irish."

We sat adjacent to a window that looked onto Beach Street. Silky caps of cream slowly melted in our dark, sweet coffee. Maria's quiet was extraordinarily different that night because it was not the smouldering silence of hot concentration, but the silence of *weltschmerz*, or unfocused weariness, which would make more sense, since she had every reason to be weary. I framed small questions, freighted with ambiguity, intending to draw out the source of her melancholy, the way one gingerly taps upon the apartment door of someone he has never met, but whom it has become absolutely essential to see.

"I suppose I am weary," she said, "but by tomorrow I'll feel differently. I'll be back to work again. It's just that now, at this precise moment, I don't see how I can possibly continue. When I'm not swept up in it, I'm tired of the whole thing. Spinach, spinach, spinach. You've been wonderful. You're probably pretty damn tired of it, too. Can't wait for this to finish."

"Just so you can get on to other things, that's all," I said. "I see the book as complete, for all intents and purposes. It's just the physical labor that is left and that pales in comparison to the earlier days, the real creation, when it was fresh and full of mysteries."

"Yes," a horn blew and she involuntarily turned her head in its direction, "but it's the continuing part that bothers me. I mean, what's next? This will be done, and there'll have to be something new. But what? I can't see it. It feels as if I'm farming the land until all the nutrients are gone. What will grow next?"

"You can't jump ahead; things'll get jumbled and nothing will work. It's like not getting out of bed one morning because you can't imagine death, or what will happen there. You're contemplating a Nothing."

"But the things I do see," she continued, "are the hard things, the arduous things. I see right now, where I am, and from this point I can see the end of this work. It's getting larger and more believable. But in this same spot, when I look backward to the point where it all started, that great expanse, I think, 'God, do you want to start way back there again, another journey of days and nights and months and months?' It's all ridiculous; that's what it is."

"Today it's ridiculous, " I said. I reached across to touch

her hand, but she did not see and pulled it away to lift her glass. "I hate it when it's ridiculous," she said, sipping her coffee. It left a trim of cream along her upper lip. She wiped it away with a swipe of her tongue. "I hate when I feel this is ridiculous, because if *this* becomes absurd, what's that make everything else?"

What indeed?

She was back to work the next day, but these gems of resumed habit were embedded in a new, burnished, spectacular foundation. Whereas before she would start placidly, wading in farther and farther until she was ultimately submerged in a flood of sustained, frenzied creativity, now she bounded in, attacked the book, threw herself into the melee. She seemed quite manic at times, a concomitance, no doubt, between her physical self and her acute mental condition. She was belligerent toward inanimate objects and bodily functions; they conspired to slow her down. The oven took too long to heat, the mail was reprehensibly slow to arrive, water from the spigot did not get hot quickly enough for her. Her agitation, long hours, poor eating habits, and thoughtless cigarette intake peaked and culminated, as best I could deduce, in a bout of diarrhea, the demands and constraints of which nearly drove her mad. (She did not admit exactly what was troubling her when I inquired, but her actions—a sudden facial contortion, an uncomfortable shifting and dancing, a desperate flight to the bathroom—made things pretty plain.) It was the only time I had ever known her to be afflicted with anything. Otherwise I cannot remember a single sneeze.

The physical world incensed her, was constantly chafing at her. She could not decide if it was a spiteful, conniving adversary standing between her and the object of her desire, or a clumsy, inept dullard, a pottering little brother that one is obliged to take along wherever she goes.

She peeled off pages dense with symbols. My typing speed doubled in a little over a two-week period, but since her dictation speed tripled, this achievement was nullified and went unnoticed by her. Even if I could have managed to type faster, my manual Underwood—enormous, slate gray, valiant—could not have sustained such speed, would have locked in a pileup of tangled hammers. Thus, another source of irritation for Maria.

She had to constantly halt and repeat lines, and no matter how diligently she tried to slow down, her momentum always carried her off into a chattering, punctuationless realm.

"Could you go back to that part about—"

"Jesus, can't you type any faster? 'Go back, go back.'"

"If indeed I were Christ, I could probably type faster."

"We'll just have to get you an electric typewriter, a word processor perhaps."

"Perhaps. We'll have to get me some money first," I said.

"Where did you stop?"

It was true: we were running low on funds. The winter layoff, the increased market trips—ofttimes for outrageously expensive ingredients; white truffles, balsamic vinegar, saffron threads—had forced me to siphon off some of my meager savings. But I was not unduly concerned, for in my daily exposure to her book, I felt reassured that more money would come from somewhere. There were, after all, three chapters floating around out there in the rarefied air of "significant others." And we were now so near completion that even I felt the spur dig in, the impetus of the looming visibility of her objective. My fingertips tingled, my head itched. My only misgiving about our furious progress lay in Maria herself. She might, in her creative delirium, her cerebral electrical storms, explode in a violent flash and bang, leaving only the detritus of tattered clothing, confetti and mangled utensils in her wake.

"The ultimate aim of Art is to enchant, enrich and instruct. Not just the reader, but the artist as well. You've got to slow down," I said as she paced, a bent elbow socketed in her palm, a glowing cigarette held up before her face like a dim beacon, a warning to approaching mariners. "This pace is unhealthy and therefore counterproductive."

"I'd like to know how you can talk and type at the same time?"

"Let's not be contentious."

"And let's not be motherly. Now if we don't finish this penultimate chapter tonight, mon ami, I may cut your heart out while you sleep."

"Maria, it would be a formality, as you already have my heart."

She stopped and gave me a blank, pendulous look for a fat moment or two, then twisted out her cigarette in a crowded obsidian ashtray and continued her dictation.

We finished the penultimate chapter (though it was really

the antepenultimate, since she still had the preface to concoct) and even proceeded onto the next before Maria stopped, swallowed two aspirin she had extracted from a tiny japanned tin, and flopped down on the bed for a few hours sleep. That purblind pumping, however, that emanates from my chest and is sometimes audible in the incredibly cavernous solitude of my studio in the A.M. as I compose this is mere illusion: the echo of an organ caroming around my vacant pericardium.

In contrast to the anxiousness, the expectation, the unwaning momentum that suffuses an arduous, painstaking task when it approaches a foreseeable completion are the hesitating half steps and behemothic silences that afflict me as this work begins winding down. I find myself lapsing into meditations, dallying over sentences, as if to postpone the inevitable. When I began this memoir, I placed the completed pages facedown next to my typewriter and paid them no mind. They were strips of flesh meticulously sliced away and left to graft, to find some type of shape, solidity, and independent life; the words and memories were a condensed, congealed manifestation of whatever it was that had drawn me to write this in the first place. I had no intention of reinjecting that which had been so artfully exsanguinated. But now I return to the text time and again, reappraising episodes and relishing old moments. My rereading, in fact, is in inverse proportion to the time I now spend actually writing, writing that was undertaken and justified from the start as a penitent act, a reconciliation, a daring and dangerous attempt to avoid perdition.

The outcome instead is something quite different, and something quite extraordinary, I think. For rather than sweeping the cobwebs from the ceiling, I have constructed an adjacent, duplicate room altogether, a new habitat, a parallel world in which I live this life once again, a streamlined bit of architecture with corners more delicately drawn, with ornamentation more decorous in its conciseness, now that excessive frills and fleurs-de-lis have been expunged, a hiding place with spaces far more elegant and economical. The ceiling above is a rondure and I sit, my arms folded, my head tilted back, and gaze comfortably at the fresco I have painted there. I admire my choice of pigments, and as they are still moist, I can alter those which appear a shade or two off. I take pleasure, feel safe, beneath the fine curvature, the gradual shifting of depicted scenes: the young Maria smiling sardonically in a Christmas dress with scalloped lace along the sleeves and neckline, flanked by large, stuffed animals; the calm, composed Maria soothing a nervous Violet; the cagey, enigmatic Maria thoughtlessly releasing a cigarette butt over the balcony rail with not the slightest interest in its path through space, in what it will see there, in where it will end. Intermittent blanks remain; there are areas of plaster still white, wet, and malleable, areas that I must yet fill. I have more work to do. I do not want to leave here . . .

A letter for Maria arrived, then another, the contents of which I was not made privy to for several days, though I knew their source and imagined their gist. The envelopes, their serrated edges peeping out from beneath a stack of books on the desk, revealed the addresses of literary agents, the "significant others," as necessary yet nevertheless as obtrusive as rain. These missives laid partially concealed for several days before Maria finally acknowledged them, though she purposely left them exposed for me to espy, maybe hoping their implication would sink in before she hazarded to discuss them. Perhaps at the time they meant something more to her than finding a publisher for her book. Perhaps they were markers for other transitions, other changes that were destined to be evinced in me. One Saturday afternoon, as she proofread the typescript, she suddenly pulled them out and began reading them, pacing the room.

"This one," she said, waving a trifolded letter, "is terribly fawning. Almost insincere. Though I was under the impression that this firm was reputable."

"And the other?" I asked.

Her face was shrouded in shadow, a penumbra of sunlight glimmered around her head.

"The other . . . the other 'likes the bend of my book,' unquote. But other than that noncommittal vagary, it sounds rather astute."

"Probably in your best interest," I said calmly, too calmly, as if these types of negotiations were common to me, "to correspond with both, don't you think?"

"Correspond? Oh no, I'm going to New York to see them, mon ami."

Pinked by this pronouncement, I no doubt went a bit white, for she fixed a queer, examining look on me for several moments, then turned her attention back to her pages. I had mixed feelings about the possible publication of her book, even though that was what we had been striving for all along. But publication in book form did not fall within the lexicon of my experience; it was not the logical end to my creative processes. Anxiety, rejection, grief, and renewed diligence were more in keeping with my work. And though we work with publication as the next natural step, as the real conclusion to an ideal craft, we don't expect it; instead we grow ambivalent toward it, and perhaps even begin to shun it. The idea of *Spinacea oleracea* finding its way into print left me nonplussed. The thought that such an occurrence would take her away from me for even the briefest time, however, was abhorrent. It sickened me, rang a dull death knell in the back of my brain. It appeared to me quite suddenly—there in my chair, open book staring up at me, muscles twitching in my etiolated face—to be a vulgarity, a corruption, a destructive act that must be avoided at all costs. Yet I remained silent as a stone.

When *Spinacea oleracea* was finally published, it fell under vigorous criticism. Although the consensus of the silly lot of critics was, on the whole, negative, so many words were expended in even the lukewarmest of receptions that the book-buying public's interest was piqued. Lengthy dismissals and denunciations of the book contributed more to its financial success than brief, affirmative notices. It shared the front page of a certain eastern Sunday book supplement with another food history that might have been a success in its own right at another time and place. Maria's monstrous work reduced it to a quaint, amateurish miniature.

Accumulating as many appraisals from that time as I could lay my hands on, I tallied up affirmatives and negatives. Many fell into an inconclusive middle ground, and my placing of some of these into a yea or nay column is purely a judgment call, and one that may swing another way entirely should I sit down again to reread and reclassify these clippings that are yellowing in an old folder. I found a curious, though not entirely surprising, pattern. Food critics and epicures, those who make a living by evaluating cooks and their books, shared the queer commonality of finding it either "excessive" or "narrow," depending on their own conceits (though I have the notion that many of them were torn between these two criticisms, and discreetly flipped a coin under the cover of their VDTs). Said one: "We come to prepare and eat food, not to praise it," an asinine assertion and one that no doubt merely glanced off Maria. A self-styled gourmet, an innovator in his own right, proclaimed, "When writing of food, we want to incite people to cook, to provide them with fodder when they feel adventuresome, and reward them for their daring. Ms. Perpetua is so incessantly championing, applauding, pitying, vindicating and bowdlerizing spinach's attitude, appearance, texture, behavior and overall mediocrity that one begins to feel she is trying to convince herself, as well as us, of something that is just not true. This reviewer does not feel that Ms. Perpetua attempted so many as half of these recipes, but simply conceived them and put them forth, like matters theological that can be supported only because they can't be disproven . . ." I call that, my position as informed source notwithstanding, hogwash.

And finally another eminent culinarist, while uncharacteristically polite, epitomized the naysayers: ". . . it is an exercise sonata, the work of a stuttering songbird; a Johnny One Note of a book. Although sometimes exquisite and inspired, showing an inkling of shading here, a hint of complexity there, it is nevertheless one note, despite its pretensions. It is water filling a balloon, threatening to burst but never quite doing so, never exploding its sack of structure and subject." A good editor might have thrown a sack over these flailing metaphors. But quite aside from that, the fallacy of such an argument is obvious. Why should a work, pure in conception and iron in purpose, stray from its framework? When a book betrays its intentions, it subsequently undermines itself. Why wander from a particular realm unless one feels that realm is insufficient as a subject, incapable of sustaining the reader's interest throughout an entire book? And if this is indeed the case, then the choice of subject itself is a mistake, and any tangential meandering is an open admission of this mistake. That *Spinacea oleracea* is thoroughly uncompromising in terms of its subject is its beauty.

Maria's book also had a decidedly positive camp of reviewers, and its members were made up mostly of critics and theoreticians of "modern literature." They found her prose beguiling, her admixture of history, lore, humor, and "quasiphilosophical musings" enchanting, controlled, and her book an all-around "good read." What is unfortunate in these favorable and ofttimes-effusive analyses is that the reviewers found the recipes, the actual formulas, anecdotal, slight interruptions to the flow of the prose. One even went so far as to admit that "so delighted was I with her 'narrative' that a third of the way through [*Spinacea oleracea*] I automatically began skipping over the recipes and sated myself on her savory prose alone." Such an assertion, I fear, probably nettled Maria more than the carping of her detractors.

Only one critic, a staff writer for an ultraliberal eastern publication, seemed to place the book in its proper perspective: "Her prosody is, by turns, titillating, addictive, and charming; rich with subtleties, puns and sly pasticcio. But when I stopped at a passage and actually made a pertinent recipe (I consumed quite a bit of spinach in preparation for this writing), the full glory of her ideas and observations opened. Suddenly an odd turn of phrase, baroque on the surface, admirable in its own queer way, but, I thought, unnecessarily obscure, acquired— with the efficacious concoction before me—depth and meaning far beyond the sheen of words, and established a special bond between she and I [sic], one that filled me with the delight of intellectual recognition."

Presuming to know what would please her, presuming to know how she intended the book to be read, I am inclined to say that that last evaluation is closest to home, is the one that may have elicited a sigh. And yet I do not know if she read any of these. The first and last review, the one of paramount importance, was her own, and hers alone. She returned from New York, by her own design, with an agent, a publisher, but nary a penny. For by sacrificing the luxuries and assurances of a publisher's advance, Maria possessed the autonomy to hold the book back until it had achieved the proper form she had envisioned for it. Not that it could in any complete way conform to her original, ideal conception of it (for what does, in this haphazard, imperfect world, attain the pure, uncontaminated shape that evolves in the uncluttered, germless vacuum of our minds, where extenuating circumstances are unable to thrive, where the cumbersome ambiguity of language and physical action is nonexistent, and where our ideas and intentions—the book, the poem, the meal, our offspring—are not yet fact, but instead a brilliant, unsullied bit of light burning in the back of our brains?), but she was determined that the book would not see print until it was as close as it could possibly be to her stringent conceptions. A monetary commitment to a publisher, then, was an unacceptable arrangement to her, one that would destroy the integrity of the work. So when they offered her an advance, with another large bit of remuneration upon delivery of the finished manuscript, Maria politely declined, saying that even a dollar was a commitment of backbreaking proportions. They balked, feeling that she intended to negotiate with some other publisher, and offered her more. Maria gave them a verbal guarantee of publishing rights, if indeed she decided to publish, and they in turn promised her an even-tidier sum upon eventual delivery.

She had still yet to write that elusive preface, that confounding, final garnish, so her work was incomplete. She did not intend the introduction necessarily as an overview, or a preparation for the reader of all that was to follow, but as self-analysis, self-critique. The process of writing it became a form of self-evaluation which she used to decide (and we know what she ultimately decided) whether or not to release the book to the wild and capricious elements of the world. Maria, like so many of us, was of the "I-Don't-Know-What-I-Think-Until-I-See-What-I-Say" school. This preface (and I see so many of you hurrying back to your copies, reacquainting yourselves with her words which are now laden—thanks to this sacred tandem of writer and reader—with meanings both real and unreal, important and inconsequential, flattened and engorged) delineates the authoress more than the text that follows. It is a frontispiece of finely penciled lines, the woman at three-quarter turn, her face poised and expressionless and slightly obscured, veiled by a translucent overlay of verbiage, a tissue to prevent the image from smearing: she is sealed beneath it. Perhaps, in the bends and shades of light and line, she saw the most agreeable reproduction of herself, the least fixed and most constantly reinterpretable image which made the photographer's proofs pale by comparison. Perhaps the absence of a jacket photo, then, is not so much an act of self-effacement, as I described it in the beginning of this memoir, as it is a display of vanity.

I am not avoiding the disquieting circumstances that fell between her decision to fly to New York and the eventual publication of her book. I am just stalking them thoughtfully, surveying the last blank area of my ceiling, patiently choosing my colors, plotting the position of my characters, securing my scaffolding so it will not fail me while I am at the most precarious point on my perch, the most conspicuous, yet dizzyingly difficult, position in my fresco. It is a depiction of paramount pain and importance, and one that would be terribly flawed should I, thoughtless from fatigue and taxed faculties, look down.

Aside from the deal she struck, I know only bits and pieces of her New York excursion. Of the unaccounted hours never alluded to, I didn't bother to ask. The whats and wheres of this time do not matter, for even the most flagrant indiscretion, the most odious and uncloaked infidelity on her part could not have increased the suffering I experienced at her absence. My pain—complete, solid, impenetrable—engulfed all possible circumstances, and none of them. It was free, unmitigated pain, unconditional and without reason, and at the same time, for every reason. It began, this stretch of strife, in the lonely hollow of my reading chair as I absorbed the full toxic force of her plan to go east, and extended—thanks to momentum—several days after her subsequent return and resettlement into her workaday habits. These were the first destructive pangs that overwhelm one who has become a victim of irretrievable loss: a hopeless, absurd, hysterical pain that is not inflicted on but unleashed within a person, one that cannot be vanquished or muted even should the person we believe to have died or defected suddenly turn up unaltered at our door. Though it seems that we would be jubilant at such a turn of events, most often we are not, because the pain has spread through us, riddled us, and fed so ravenously off the part of us that was tied to that person that the relationship is not the same, and things have changed forever.

In a green-and-white taxi—a Plymouth, I believe—we sat close to one another in the back seat. Maria stared through the drop-jeweled window at the pewter mists of the freeway, and I stared at the dandruff-dusted shoulders of the anonymous driver, worrying the fingers of Maria's tiny hand in its pretty pink glove with two waxy mother-of-pearl buttons at the wrist. Her dress was also pink, with a dropped waist that obscured the curving line of her feminine form and gave her the epicene shape of a frail, prepubescent girl. She wore a long single strand of pearls, whose authenticity I doubted but dared not inquire about, and her face, in the strange, muddled, rainy light of the cab, had the same nacreous pallor: a colorlessness from weeks of sequestered composition. She was without expression or emotion, displaying neither excitement nor happiness over the prospect of the four days that lay ahead. I could discern, from my maddening scrutiny and irritating reiteration of "What's wrong; is anything wrong?", nothing about her mood. As an escort, I was impotent. Her stoicism was impenetrable. And although the last thing I wanted to see was Maria boarding her plane, I longed in my simple insecurity for her departure, the calling of her flight, just for the very good-bye it would require, the telltale good-bye that we would share. For I hoped to glean from it either a hopeful or, heaven help me, a forbidding simulacrum of the future.

Checking her baggage with the clerk, I thought of the manuscript within, cloaked in an incalculable mess of clothes. Her book: that constant irritant and splendid gem, possibly the only authentic pearl on her person, the critical density of her life amassed on pages, nestled in the deceiving integument of absurd fluff. As I waited there on the curb, I saw Maria through the brief parting of the pneumatic doors gazing pie-eyed at a board of departing flights, her hand slowly patting the shiny pink purse at her hip, and I realized that the fact she was without some of her belongings—her clothes acquired from different roommates, and different lodgings, her inquiline accumulations, her stocks and reserves, her obscure literary/culinary tomes, her epicurean instruments—meant nothing, for they had all been coddled, clarified and incorporated into her book, the sum total of her life until that point, the influence, advice, and acquiescence of yours truly included. It needed not even its originator to give it life, to actualize it, for it was already actualized. Pounds of sweat and flesh had been expended in the process of giving it life, in making it breathe, and a trillion or more electrical impulses had been fired in its construction. Now it pulsed, radiated, throbbed in my hand, a new organism, the accumulated tissue of an identity, but one far less flawed, since it had been combed of abnormalities, of capricious genetic unpredictables, of deep-seeded, unforeseen mutations. It was an item in bloom *ad infinitum*, as pure and perfect in form as she could possibly make it at this stage, forged from the finest genes of her patience, her pullulating intellect, her superfecund praxis. The clerk stapled a claim check to her ticket, handed it back to me, and placed her suitcase—a precocious child, a mischievous, bright-eyed savant, a living thing—amidst a variety of inanimate, insignificant others.

"Your flight is nonstop, you know," I took her arm.

"Of course," she said, meaning, I suppose, that she would not have otherwise cast her manuscript to the indifferent winds of baggage handlers. And yet, knowing her as I think I do, I felt sure a twin existed somewhere, safe in those desk drawers I dared not open or perhaps already on the launching pad of some publisher's desk in New York.

As I walked with her through the wide, streamlined regions of the terminal, a strange feeling of loneliness and desolation crept over me. It was as if she had already gone, taken flight, and I were simply accompanying or witnessing an after-image: the bright bits of evidence that a comet has passed or a sun set; those glimmering flecks and luminous arches of color that still stain the vacant sky; or the fragmented, auriferous line of a vapor trail glowing over a sunless horizon, disjointed and seemingly self-candescent, self-sustaining, like the crushed and smeared phosphor of a firefly. But quite unlike the firefly's tail, the light and color in this case was solely dependent upon another, far greater source of energy to give it definition and existence. For the bands of color crisscrossing the sky are ephemeral, without form, a projected phenomenon of something too complex to keep itself to itself. A shadow seen alone is simply nothing suggesting something, but if that something constantly eludes us, lets us see no more than its shadow bending about corners and ducking through doorways, then what do we have?

I felt that I had, in effect, inauspiciously and unwittingly parted from her. As I stepped aside to avoid one of those beeping, electric-powered shuttle carts bearing down on us (driven by a mad-eyed porter who appeared to be imagining himself in a milieu other than a pedestrian-crowded airport), my expectations about our good-bye were blunted, my desire to see her stay was crushed, and my need to be home and alone to lament these confusions and metaphysical conflicts was profound and impatient.

She had already secured her boarding pass, and as we reached her gate, I—preoccupied, distracted, forlorn—took her sheathed hand, brushed my lips against it, and quietly asked her to please call me as I began backing away, nearly treading on the sneakered toes of a small, shapely blond woman in a snug Grateful Dead jersey who was eating a handful of raisins, and who gave me a comic, slightly exophthalmic look of surprise and derision. And my farewell—bungled, brief—seemed to startle Maria. It did not fit the variety of likely scenarios she had perhaps half-consciously envisioned. For the first time in the entire text of our actions and interactions, I acted in a way she had not foreseen. I did not loiter over sentimental inanities, nor linger by way of unconvincing, woolgathering chatter, fussing over her appearance or reciting a superfluous list of Now-Don't-Forgets. Nor did I, on the other extreme, affect some cool, rational detachment, the ultimate camouflage for rent, hopeless romantics who remain icily composed until they reach the lugubrious void of their doubly silent room, then throw themselves on the bed in a protracted fit of hysterics and grief. Unlike these caricatures and their variants, I merely faded eerily away. And Maria, her gloved hand dangling before her like a fantoccini's, remained transfixed as I disappeared amidst the other passengers.

I returned to my digs with the haste of a man fleeing assassins and sat in the silent half-light. I tried to stop the intrusion of life, to create a tank of deprivation where my abject silence would be right at home, where it would project no dimension and have no surface. It had been my hope, I suppose, to suppress my senses and thus smother my sensibilities. If I could successfully achieve such a condition, I imagined, I might then reduce my silence and my sadness (habitual silence! horrid sadness!) to pure irrelevance, insignificance, or, ideally, nonexistence. I cared to be a mere consciousness aware only of itself, an absolute energy in an infinite area—something outside of glum Time, unconstricted by tyrannical Space—and vault my petty station of poet mourning his muteness, lover lamenting his loss.

But such escape was doomed to failure, for no matter how effectively I stayed the entrance of lights, sights, and sounds, life leaked in and pooled around me. From the street, the corridor, came the pops, whooshes, rumbles, beeps, and the occasional unrhythmic dactyls of unintelligible conversations of the outside world. I plugged my ears, but this induced a more maddening, distant roar, as if a wind were rising in my skull, and this was shortly followed by the heavy booted two-step of my heart. Despite drawn blinds and closed doors, a mouse-colored light, dulled by rain, spilled through cracks and around corners. A thread of light gleamed in the prismatic lip of an ashtray; it illuminated a solitary table leg; it rubbed a soft luster into the nummular face of a doorknob. It penetrated just enough to provide an anemic definition to the room. And even with my eyes tightly closed, the dim iridial halos, and the luminous snakes of my capillaries confirmed, emphasized, the very physical presence I had hoped to transcend.

What was this silence of such great proportion, so physically enervating and emotionally moiling that I should not care even to address it, that I should want to reduce its quantity to the point of utter inconsequence, that I could not even bear it in the friendly and familiar sanctuary of my rooms? If it had been only the simple speechlessness of surprise, or the confusion of one who finds his routine amended and his shadow absent, or even the wordlessness of a writer, the inarticulate dullness of one who knows precisely what he must say but just cannot bring himself to say it, then I'd have had nothing to fear; these silences were not foreign to me. They had infected me before, and though they were never pleasant, neither were they chronic; they could be assuaged with any number of tried and tested anodynes. True, my poetic silence had lasted far longer than what seemed healthy, and my Vietnam poem still lay in state, a victim of clashing with Maria's abortifacient energies, but even that (I barely gave it a thought) was insufficient to leave me so angst ridden. My silence was the portent of terror, and my terror was the anticipation of loneliness. In my projections of the present, I saw nothing. Or rather I saw myself, but not the me of the past, not the pre-Maria me when I had possessed, despite solitude and anonymity, a doppelgänger that encompassed all the elements of my life: my job, my poetry, my concubine, the muse Calliope, the vice of mild hallucinogens, the tranquility of smug vanity. I had been my own companion, my own foil, my own concern. I had lived the onanistic sin of the artist. Until Maria.

For Maria, a far more intransigent agent of this sin, far more ruthless, far less penitent, far less swayed, was precisely like me in every respect but one: She had not invested, nor had she ever intended to invest, her unconditional love in me. I was a piece of her solipsistic world as Yvette had been a piece of mine. But through some aberration, through some deficiency in my usually steadfast, self-serving soul, I had let things run amok and had abandoned my passion for myself so that I might possess her. Had I never seen her, I thought, I would not have felt the terror I felt that day, but that was not true. I was destined to see her; it was preordained, a test of the muses, who, having served me unstintingly for so long, had decided it was time to see if I was really worthy of their aid, if I had the heart and mind of a legitimate artist, impervious to earthly distraction and hardy enough to withstand the hostile environment beyond my ivory tower. And I failed. I betrayed them. I took the gifts they had given expressly to me and cast them at the feet of another.

The past several months were laid bare, sliced, pinned back and bisected like a junior biologist's pickled frog, and the foul deterioration beneath the otherwise-unblemished skin issued forth; the malignant past was identified and the bleak future foreseen. My shrouded room manifested what existed beyond: a world of darkness and flickering light that we grope through blindly, barking our shins and banging our heads on shapes that were once clearly limned, but are now incomprehensible and frustrating; we feel like the stroke victim whose reading faculties have been thoroughly destroyed, or the amputee who still grimaces from phantom pain. The brain, in its nostalgic, optimistic momentum, persists in sending out commands for action but, finding no outlet, they travel the Möbius strip of what is left of us.

I found myself outdoors, in the damp and fetid air, in the relentless mist of that murky Saturday, heading—a tropism drove me on toward the old purlieu of more prolific days—to visit Yvette. I hoped that she would not be there. I hoped to find, upon inquiry, that she had left some time before with an oil man, a wealthy financier, or best of all, an orthopedic surgeon who'd perfected a revolutionary corrective technique.

The house where Yvette worked occupied the top two floors of a century-old tobacconist's shop. The windows were dark, the drapes drawn, the ladies most likely well into their second stage of sleep, it still being only midmorning. A small woodcut sign bearing decussated pipe stems above a tiny humidor swung weakly from S-hooks above the shop door. The street was empty but for some parked cars and a jogger who huffed by in shiny black shorts and a windbreaker and gave me, I thought, a smarmy look (sizing me up perhaps as some nicotine addict and thus morally inferior). Recessed from the sidewalk, next to the tobacconist's entrance, was another door, the one leading up into that rich maze of remembered delights, as inconspicuous as any apartment door, with its ornately paraphed street number—a half number greater than the street-level shop—painted a ruby red. In the door frame was an orange illumined button—a socketed baby aspirin—that activated the buzzer within, which was really the muted yipping of an office telephone. Madame Nerval (a pseudonym plucked from her favorite poet) would open the electric door, giving one entrance to the stairwell, at the top of which was another door, where our housemother would identify the visitor through a sliding speakeasy panel. One had to be recognized to get in, or be accompanied by a regular, and if nothing was amiss or out of the ordinary, if the patron was not grossly inebriated or wretchedly unkempt, then Mme Nerval would escort him to a drawing room where he would reside until his preferred princess was unoccupied.

The drawing room was a sumptuous, Victorian affair, rich with slick, varnished mahogany, scarlet velveteen draperies, a shelved wall buttressed with cloth-bound books, and a panoply of vases and gewgaws, watercolors and statuettes. A Louis Quatorze étagère held a lacquered cigarette box replenished daily with fresh, gold-tipped Sobranies. A scroll-armed sofa with leonine legs was upholstered in a pale hyacinth chintz, dotted with delicate, cinnamon, trefoil flowers. A waist-high, marble-topped table displayed a reproduction of a Fabergé egg, roughly the size of a large avocado, frilled and trimmed, dense with bijouterie: jade dentate leaves, rows of turquoise crockets, gimmaled ringlets of opalescent asteria, incised gold petals surrounding emerald stigmas, and topped with a sterling spindle that needled to a lethal-looking point at its apex. The egg's upper hemisphere tilted back and upon a small circular stage (thanks to a brass, valentine-shaped key at the back base), a nacreous-faced girl and a centaur danced and rotated in a dreamlike, hypnotic lentissimo minuet. The egg was accessible to all; gentle examination and fingertip scrutiny were permissible (so impeccable were Mme Nerval's clients that the egg's public display was a compliment to her keen assessment of character), not only because of the genuine pleasure it gave her to see it cooed over and admired, but also (she informed me when I queried her once over its prominent place and general lack of security) because the lilt and sweetness of the terpsichorean twosome had a tranquilizing effect on customers and put them in a mind frame appropriate to the tune and tenor of the House.

Scattered elsewhere were one or two Ming vases, a long-jawed, baying, lupinelike fetish, an ethereal Monet of misty water lilies in a gilt, rococo frame, a lamped lectern with a magnifying glass in a felt-lined nook and an OED opened (unless a browser had call to look something up) to the page which bore "Eros" (and on the opposite page, though I was not tasteless or foolhardy enough to bring it to Madame's attention, "ersatz"). On a low table adjacent to a wing chair was a large portfolio album, updated periodically, of full-color photographs of all the girls, provocatively but not slatternly dressed, usually in lacy or silken garments, with a *curriculum vitae* on the verso (e.g., their age, their birthplace, their interests, their "favorite things"). Many patrons changed partners regularly precisely because they found this method of leisurely getting to browse and muse and linger over the myriad ladies satisfying and, as a form of fantasy fulfillment, stimulating; for who of these men had not, at least one time in his life, glimpsed a gamine in an erotic magazine or lingerie catalog and longed to possess her for the fullness of a wanton mouth, a brazen gaze, the assurance of an insinuating posture, or just to realize the mythopoetic ardor of attaining one who is photogenically exquisite and utterly anonymous?

I never strayed from Yvette, though I visited from time to time with the clear intention of doing so. But in my perusal of that book of wares, it was she who coralled and exacerbated my desire (she was reclining—the photo was discreetly cropped at her shins—on a canopy bed, veiled by translucent sheers fluttering open from an unseen, anabatic wind, like an odalisque in a harem tent. The scene had the jellied haze and soft retouching of a centerfold, with Yvette nestled amid satiny, freshly wrecked sheets with peaks and eddies as smooth as whipped cream. She wore a clingy, maraschino camisole that, in contrast to the whiteness of her skin, made her look like a sculptured piece of peppermint candy. A red fillet held back her ashen hair; her head rested on an extended arm; her right breast was just seconds away from falling free; and her look—directly at me—was one of contented lassitude and splendid fatigue.) Even when she was two or three hours from being available, I could not bring myself to sample others but would patiently wait, indulging in the intellectual attractions of the drawing room, biding my time with one of Mme Nerval's many tomes (of particular interest were two queer, absurd rarities [or rare absurdities]: Lux's *Exorcism of a Hyperliterate Adolescent* and Dr. Betruger's *The Crepuscule of Antiquity*).

At this time in the morning, however, I was not about to be admitted, for as all the regulars knew, the bell was disconnected so the girls could not be disturbed, and even if I did manage to get Mme Nerval's attention, it was doubtful she would let me in because of my rain-soaked, unsavory-looking state and my absence from the premises for so many months with nary a word. Even gentlemen who desisted in frequenting the house—because of marriage or ascent to public office—still dropped by occasionally with small gifts and greetings, sent a bottle of wine or flower basket or at least a Christmas card. But I, in my months of fidelity, had gone out of my way to avoid even passing by the place. A month after Maria had moved in, I had received a postcard that bore a drawing of a tiny hourglass with its sands draining away and the preprinted message, "It's been some time since your last visit to our boutique. Won't you stop by soon?" Hastily mangling the card in angry abjuration, I thought, this is not *modus operandi* for the habitués of this little nest, and that Mme Nerval (a small but distinguished-looking woman with a pinched mouth and large clay-colored eyes that had a vocabulary all their own, particularly when they receded behind her banana-tinted pince-nez, which she wore on a lanyard and could, in moments of mock surprise or exaggerated disbelief, cause to fall away from her face with a certain slight, learned wrinkling of her nose) was unhappy with me, most likely because of something that Yvette had told her about our last, adverse encounter.

So then what to do? Standing there in the rain, my clothes wet and heavy upon me, my hair matted as soaked straw, I suppose that I did not want to encounter Yvette, (or anyone there, for that matter) so much as I simply wanted to get a look at her, or not to get a look at her, to ascertain that she had gone, fled, escaped, persevered, survived, that she had overcome her station, had fared better than I. I could stand nearby and wait, but that might mean cold countless hours without really knowing whether she remained or not. I could ring her up, but Mme Nerval would no doubt screen the call and smell a ruse.

Checking the alley, I was reminded of what I'd known all along. The building was zigzagged with a fire escape. So, as stealthily as a sedentary poet, wheezing and waddling, still half-astonished at the unwieldy impediment of his newfound corpulence, can move, I carefully extended the telescoping ladder and began my farcical, fumbling climb to the third floor, to Yvette's window.

The artist is a voyeur. The voyeur is a thief. Therefore the artist is a thief, for being a voyeur, he robs his subjects of their intimacy; he negates it, draws out their privacy with two incredibly rapacious, insatiable eyeballs. But if the voyeur is present, and intimacy is then absent, is that really theft? If intimacy is not there, then how can the voyeur purloin something that does not exist? Or, if the subject is unaware of the voyeur, if the subjects of this clandestine scrutiny still believe that they possess their privacy and continue to act accordingly, if they are not restricted, hampered in their actions because the presence of the voyeur is unknown, is intimacy really nullified? Is it taken away; are habits and movements blunted? No, no, what you don't know might not hurt you; what you don't know may even help you, may even ennoble you in the eyes of, and thanks to, the discreet usurper and fractional villain. For, by your ignorant innocence, you are better than he; you have devalued him simply by your unsuspecting presence; you have diminished him in the scheme of the moral universe (if indeed he too inhabits this universe). You may even save his black-edged, putrifying soul from further damnation, may shock him into humble, weak-kneed repentance, as he—alone, utterly alone and unseen—finds himself in the cranny of his own chrysalid malfeasance, lined with evincible mirrors and void of ventilation so that he may see in the rondure of reflection his freakish permutations and whiff the thick, unaerated stench of his deterioration.

O, what did I want to see, what did I hope to attain, ambling up, up, my footfalls gently thringing and bonging almost inaudibly on those iron rungs and slippery black gratings? Fat limaciform smudges and indelible black spots? The unwanted presence on an overdue X ray? Pinpricks and perforations?

I saw myself, a wet and wild-eyed reflection, until I cupped my hand to the grimy glass and, through the crescent eclipse of my crazed countenance, looked into her room. On the wall directly across from me, the stubs of two stick candles burned low in the sockets of a tarnished girandole, in the gleaming, convex center of which I glimpsed myself glimpsing, distant and diminished, as in the wide-ranging reflection of the department-store mirrors used to thwart shoplifters. To my right, on the bed against the wall, was Yvette, unquestionably Yvette, spread-eagled atop her mattress, her modest, bone-shade peignoir bunched immodestly around her waist, her hand extended over the edge of the bed and curled around the neck of a liquor bottle. I thought I could hear the baffled air of quiet snoring. On the nightstand next to her was a fused, multicolored lump of spent candles, in the midst of which one vermicular wick still survived and sustained a faintly guttering flame as small as a sucked lemon drop. On the floor below me, along with blouses and various undergarments, was one black shoe with a forbidding, built-up sole, its lashing tongue volute, curled in disgust, its black laces angrily sinuous, as alive and choking as unattended vines. Seeing it forced free a squeaky sob from my throat, and as I reached back to steady myself, my elbow whacked the iron railing, which rang out with a low gloomy resonance. Yvette sat up quickly, but the sharp movement and sudden shift in elevation afflicted her with such a piercing throb that she dropped back down, moaning, waiting for her fermented brain to repressurize. For several seconds she looked at the hand that held the bottle, as if she were willing it to approach her lips, but it simply dangled from her fingers until she let it fall to the floor with a thunk. Gin pooled spatulate on the carpet.

Yvette pushed herself up, swung her legs over the other side of the bed, and hobbled—doubly encumbered—to her dressing table, where she sat before the mirror and raked her fingers through the impossible knots of her hair. Her face was haggard and white—not the former white of bisque, but of paste—and her eyes were small and red as cranberries. The darkness beneath them defined the waning phases of twin moons. Dehydration from drink had dried her lips and etched them with streamlets of cracks, and at the corner of her mouth in low relief was a cold sore that she gingerly touched with her forefinger, its presence forgotten in stuporous sleep but now lividly remembered and lamented. However long ago it had erupted, that was how long Yvette had surely been quarantined from customers—who tend to become understandably hesitant at the sight of such things—her picture temporarily removed from the book so as not to disappoint anyone, her meals brought to her by another girl, her evenings spent shut in her rooms listening to the muffled footsteps, the opening and closing doors, the barely distinguishable, slightly inhuman emanations from rooms around and below, the flushing of toilets, the distant buzzer, the pedestrian traffic, the vague, uncertain, glassy tinkle of the tobacconist's bell coming up through her open window, the flat monophonic music of Haydn and Elgar and Saint-Saëns from her weak transistor. As interminable as incarceration. A healing time for the body but not much instauration for the spirit. A period that clamored for imbibition.

Still drunken and probably neurasthenic, she quaked with a few dry sobs, then cradled her face in her hands. Mea culpa, O mea culpa, I wanted to cry, to tumble through the window and take her, weeping, in my damp and trembling arms. The crushing thumb of solitude and loss of solicitude had so infected and riddled her, had proven so devastating that a patulous pressure of despair spread through my chest, and a finger-wagging humility chastised me for the comparative triviality of my own agitations. Enough, I had seen enough, I could stay there no more at the risk of committing some regrettable act.

But I hung on just a few extra moments. She rose feebly

from her dressing table, hoisted herself up on slim white arms, shuffled to the girandole, extinguished the candles—which would have facilitated their own expiration in another few moments—and saw there my own mottled, gelid and frightening reflection. Her head pivoted, her lips curled back in horror, her eyes expanded wide and round as brass buttons, and she emitted a shriek that eviscerated me, sent me reeling backward, butted me up against the railing where the weight of my upper body propelled me over and I flailed with legs and arms to take hold of something, anything, but my momentum cast me clear of anything to grip. It was the end. I would expire, a hideous, oozing doll, face down in an alley. And queerly, my toppling into unbroken space seemed protracted, half-speed, slow enough for me to experience the terrifying, unearthly frissons and throat-constricting impotency of a solid mass in an insubstantial environment—a gemstone plopped into a cup of oil. I saw (my eyes open? Closed? It doesn't matter) not my life but perhaps (for I have not yet decided) a phantasmic allegory of it: arcs of light melting through shades of the spectrum, swinging beams forming luminous pentagrams, splitting like cells, clustering and swelling until finally giving way to the shimmering image of Violet falling backward from the coffee table to the couch. It was as impalpable as the air around me and played over and over again repeatedly, but with each successive descent faster than the last, accelerating in proportion to my velocity until, at my nadir, it was but an indistinguishable and irritating flicker that I wished would cease. And as quickly as my mind could articulate that desire, it did.

I was swallowed by darkness. Death was outrageously easy. In my blushing giddiness over my strange new state, I thought to my dead self, if I could now only tell Yvette how pitifully simple and satisfying it is, how the only fear is a false one instilled in us by Life—a greedy essence wholly separate from our soul—that, so hysterical over losing us, enacts a horrifying, histrionic deception, trying to convince us that *we* are losing something that in actuality we do not need nor ever really possessed. Life was a notion, a quaint bit of theory, and we made it an entity by our very existence. We fed this notion—overfed it—and then, as it loomed larger and larger, we sanctified it, deified it, assigned it a value greater than that of man *en masse*, concocted laws to protect it, established ineffable myths and ornate institutions to pay homage to it. We let it govern us: a brain wave of a nanosecond, a dream, a sneeze in the dark, the emperor's new clothes, an imaginary yoke tossed over all the snorting, rutting chaos . . .

But Death? Why Death was undemanding and understanding, tranquil and demulcent as a melody, as efficacious as a mild narcotic. It did not proselytize, it needed no agitprop, it affected no grandeur. We Think, Therefore It Is, and for that polite gesture on our part, Death is unassuming, grateful and compensatory. Thank you very much, welcome to the region of your own making, please make yourself quite at home, excuse the smell.

The smell? Yes. For all its soothing softness and transitional ease, Death certainly had a gaminess to it, an offal aroma that nearly made my soul gag. And as I pondered the source of this stink, I suddenly heard voices. Could we speak to one another here?

"He was up there," said a voice with distant familiarity. But whose? An old forgotten aunt? A deceased grade-school teacher?

"Well, he got away. Not much we can do about it," said a gruff and thoroughly foreign other voice. Got away, I thought: a soul whom Life had held onto, someone who had balked at making the passage. Poor pitiable fool. Their voices trailing off, the entities moved away. I heard the gruff one say, "Just tell your girls to keep their—" and then it was gone.

My mistake registered. My stomach knotted. And true to my human form, I emerged from my camouflage of wet and reeking rubbish and vomited. A dun-colored, scrofulous tom, nosing an empty sardine tin, fled mortified down the alley.

I experienced no remorse, nor offered up any hollow gratitude to whatever had thrust a fortuitous dumpster in the path of my free-fall. What could I offer, and to whom? I was not overcome with any reverential awe, nor visited by any enlightenment, nor thankful to ambivalent deities. It was simply another interlacing in the arabesque of coincidence, another symmetry mimicked, a numerical oddity, a girl in a jump seat, the random collapse of distant suns. I would like to say that providence jolted me, that the immensity of my fortune sent me scuttling back to my rooms to write the immortal poems that would otherwise have never known existence, but it didn't. I merely picked garbage from my person, put my fetid clothes into a paper sack and dropped them down the trash chute, showered (twice—my nostrils were still incredulous about my actual cleanliness), and smoked myself into a grotesque and ravenous oblivion.

This grandiose and illogical state does not fool me. I know it for what it is. Though I can concentrate (or so it seems) my attentions down to the tiniest and most thoroughgoing ponderings, I am not deceived or deluded enough to actually believe, like some, that this state is some loquacious latitude of insightful eloquence. Who would, after all, want to read an epic poem on microbes, or the animal shapes that can be found in pieces of popped corn? No, I stay clear of pen and paper when under hashish's blustery influences.

The insignificant, however, bloats and burgeons with outrageous importance. Emotions grow preposterous. We become junior psychoanalysts. The abandoned correspondence with an old school chum, a harsh and unkind word we said to our mother when we were nine years old, the carnival prize of a plastic dog tethered to a slender tube that leaps and yaps from air bursts administered by a rubber squeeze ball become by our ridiculous and convoluted reasoning, the linchpins and keystones of the state of our current psyche. The insignificant holds massive secrets to our enormous existence.

And when we have regained an everyday state of mind, we laugh off these dissertations as the folderol they are. We vigorously reject them as the senseless sirocco of a hallucinating mind, and that is that. Even if we managed to finger a nerve, even if all that purple poetizing has a whitish glimmer of truth, we sluff it off and slip into a more commonsensical mien. We become "rational." We practice emotional restraint. The less wrenching, more mundane flotsam of life pops to the surface and commands our attention.

It was for this hyper and frenzied distillation, this introspective divertissement that I stayed, for the four days of Maria's absence, as frail and high as a box kite. Slay the beast that stalked my entrails; reinvent our history together, bottle it, atomize it, fill the air with its fragrance, inhale it, reel from it, die over it again and again, melodramatize the fact that she has gone so you may face her eventual going. Forearmed is forewarned.

For four days I muttered and hummed and hankered and howled, my lungs raling from smoke, my mouth as dry as flour, my eyes small as cherrystones and cobwebbed with bright swollen vessels, my apartment littered with candy wrappers, empty pretzel bags, nut jars, balls of colored foil, crumpled soda cans, stale bread heels, olive pits deposited in trays and furry with ashes. I reeled and rollicked through a farrago of imprecations, condemnations, jeremiads against any and all (except, of course, Maria) decrying my situation, my sloth, my hopeless silence, my unremunerated love. I narrated, aloud, snippets of this brief history of ours, and the actual articulation of it, hushed and falling softly in the studious stuffiness of the room, caused it to impact on me far more melancholically, with far more bittersweetness. These words, released from the quicksilver of memory and given thick and cumbersome utterance, suddenly comprised truth, and "reality." My very verbalization of them legitimized them as facts, the way a bereaved individual, in the stupefying shock of loss, finally says, "She's dead," thus turning the numbing, terrifying notion into a grievous and dementia-inducing hammerblow.

I had never before suffered loss, at least not of any consequence. Cherished possessions had disappeared or were stolen; women had left me; a companionable, much-loved cat was taken from me by two delinquents with air-rifles. But now, having for the first time in my life immersed myself, my work, my happiness, in one person, one desire, I perceived the potential for the loss of my entire world, my delicate identity, my modest contentment. The effects of this self-cloistering and then sudden abandonment of it had left me unprepared. How does one abide? How does one go on? I searched back—trying to shed new light on old days, trying to recall a sense of what I was before Maria, a sense of the regular, run-of-the-mill, work-a-day feelings I had then, of my mind's processes, of my general comportment in a world where I hadn't even an inkling that such a person as Maria Perpetua existed—but everything prior to her was tabula rasa. I could recall incidents and instances and items—a boyhood dream, a favored book, a lone moment on a windy beach, an erotic encounter. But alone, these things signified nothing. My life was the accumulation of my experiences, an edifice of interrelated beams and blocks. And the keystone to this arrangement was Maria. She held my life as the arching doorway back through which I could gaze. To remove her, in terms of introspection, would leave me with but a pile of stones.

We hadn't planned to meet at the airport, but I did want to be somewhat prepared for her return. I was dehydrated and fatigued, my body's immune system dangerously low from both the hashish and a diet of hastily eaten junk. The fluctuating and flummoxing influence of the hallucinogen distorted my sense of time. To what degree, however, was not clear to me until, immersed to my bristly chin in a bathtub of tepid, brackish water, I heard Maria thump down her bag and shut the apartment door.

There was a silence, the length of which I cannot estimate, with any accuracy. Enough time for the slight disarray to sink in. The refrigerator door must have been ajar for I heard it *thuck* closed without the suctional sound of it's having been opened. This was no calamity, I thought, in my addled insouciance, since all that remained in it were a couple of lemons with rust-colored spots, a half of a bottle of superannuated Chianti, and various condiments which I had not gotten around to consuming in my binge of ingestion.

I heard the crunching of paper, the slap of the trash can lid, the liberating clatter of a window being flung open. Followed by more silence. It was then that I was consumed with a paranoia approaching panic. I held my thin, wheezy breath. I was frightfully certain that the next sound would be the raucous final slamming of the apartment door as Maria walked away for good. All scenarios are botched, all endings are anticlimactic, all goodbyes are undramatic, I reasoned. That is why we have artists, to squeeze magic from the mundane. She would walk away, while I floated like a specimen in a jar.

But that is not what she did.

Gingerly, with flattened hand, she pushed open the bathroom door, as if she were uncertain of the nature of the beast within. I splashed a bit to assure her I was alive, but it wasn't a very spirited splash. More like a sick plop.

I squinted at her with eyes that looked, no doubt, like socketed rubies. She wore her dirndl skirt, with a crushed white cotton V-neck T-shirt, sleeves rolled above her shoulders, the fabric holding the shape of her breasts, casting them in the texture of unfinished plaster. A chignon bobbed at her nape, sprouting several strands of black gossamer that rose and fell in concert, as eerie and fluid as tentacles. The stub of a smouldering cigarette she tossed in the sink. "Mon ami?" she said, and knelt next to the tub. My eyes began to burn. I could not stop staring at her. In those four days, from the moment I had left her at the airport standing with her feet primly together and her hand outstretched, I had forgotten what she looked like. The deep darkness of her classic heroine's eyes, the pale delicacy of her throat, the close-set, cashew-colored floret of each ear. The Maria of the four days' absence was a sharper, silent thing, penetrating and maddening; not so much a flesh-and-blood woman as an angry avatar, or a brilliant, lavish, inaccessible work of art.

I closed my stinging eyes, and she leaned over and kissed me, kissed me for a very long time. Her lips tasted of wax from some gloss, her breath was hot and dangerous and exciting from tobacco. My heart bulged, there were stirrings in my bath, but as I tried to push myself up to a better position, my palms slid along the slippery bottom of the tub and I fell away from her, plunging beneath the grayish water.

EIGHT

Of the deal she struck I have already spoken. There were details pertaining to its production that still had to be worked out. She stipulated that there were to be no glossy photographs of prepared recipes. Her editors—two women, she said, roughly my age: one short, with crimped black hair, a florid nose, a slight case of adult acne, and physically shaped like an Anjou pear; the other nearly as tall as Violet, with cropped, strawberry-blond hair, a thin mouth, no breasts, and long, elegant, vermiform fingers—had suggested line drawings here and there to demonstrate the certain techniques step-by-step. Maria would only consent to illustration, she said, if they resurrected Sir John Tenniel and convinced him to work up some drawings of a dark-haired Alice "cajoling and cavorting with a grotesquerie of ladles and letters, with slithy toves and mome raths and a frumious bandersnatch or two." No doubt they found her more charming than churlish, more delightful than difficult, more enterprising than eccentric. She requested, firmly, control over the typography (the text, as one can learn from the colophon, was set in ITC Garamond Book); she would work closely with the artist on the design for the jacket. She would arrange and approve the back cover photo. She specified that the book (despite its topic), be bound in a navy-colored cloth—she detested green—with a robin's egg spine, and imprinted on the front would be simply her initials, silverish, and not her signature. No deckle edge to the pages. She also expressed her desire to have each section thumb-indexed, like a dictionary, "but that simply elicited a lot of feet-shuffling and low-whistling and snorting laughter." This last recommendation was not so important, she said. Obviously it was not honored, but she threw it in nevertheless, believing that such an extravagance would make her other directives much more palatable. These details were discussed over an extended, languorous lunch, where she had a "butterflied piece of meat, obscenely grilled, and coated with a ridiculous cognac cream sauce, dicey with peppercorns," and everyone else there took meticulous care to avoid ordering anything with spinach. When I asked her if the name of a certain poet came up in the course of conversation, she said—her head bent forward, her hands at her neck, extracting pins and freeing her thick bob of hair—that she must "put on some weight before I can begin throwing it around, mon ami."

And that weight, which she inevitably acquired, came not from anything she ingested, but instead from the public's massive consumption of *Spinacea oleracea*. It was up to her to deliver the book and the very next morning after her return, following an extended sojourn to various markets (where we restocked, at least partially, our pantry), she set about composing her exordium, the pontifical preface that up until that time had eluded her. She dissected the innumerable drafts. She skimmed, again and again, the pages of her manuscript, poured over *The Gastronomic Hejira* like a rabbinical student over the Torah. It was not with the macédoine of symbols, with fulgurant explosions of inspiration and hectic storms of creativity that she wrote the final pages of the book. It was a smouldering, plodding, ponderous parade of hours spent bent over the desk; a slow and deliberate bloodletting; an application of leaches to the soles of her feet. She would lift her head and stare into the middle distance, finding her metaperspective, assessing her shadow, and a dull ache crept into *my* joints, a pressure pushed its thumbs to *my* temples. From my chair in the corner I could only watch her, feeling forlorn, jejune, helpless, being of absolutely no assistance to her now.

She worked a sleepless forty-eight-hour period, breaking only for trips to the toilet, for glasses of water. The feast she ordained required a fast. She left the apartment but one time, to buy a legal pad because, for the first time I can remember in my life as a poet, there was not a clean sheet to be found. It made my artistic tenure apocryphal. I certainly hadn't gobbled it up, nor been recently enough near a blank page to know they were in short supply. On that excursion she also purchased a pack of cigarettes, something she had done without since beginning her preface, and even the craved nicotine was too much of an intrusion, too dithering and obfuscating a presence, a distorting poison that violated her impromptu abstinence. She cursed as the first chemical surge rushed through her veins, twisted out the butt and tossed the pack across the room.

Why did I not run her errands? Why did I remain in the lowering half-light, hyperattentive to a discordant glut of senseless sounds—a door slamming with emphatic finality, an amplified stereo strumming the floorboards, droplets plopping in the bathroom sink due to a flawed washer—identifying each,

spiraling off into near delirium, losing context, then identifying all again? Whether it was from the actual physical effects of
my four days of debauchery or something with psychological
origins, I do not know, but shortly into Maria's first full day
back in San Francisco, I became ill. My stomach churned and
squeezed out its contents. My blood, frantic to defeat some
virulence, increased its temperature. Every joint was shot with
pain. Sleep came with difficulty, by exhausting degrees, and
always ended badly. My fever and its gargoylish manifestations
jolted me into anguished consciousness. It had been so long
since I had known illness that each twinge, each throb, each
gastro-intestinal lurch heralded the end, was the beginning of
a death rattle. And I welcomed it. To leave her before she left
me! What a poetic flourish to my otherwise prosaic despair.

The beginning of the end of my fever came on the morning
I was drawn out of a frantic chase dream by a coolness applied
to my forehead. It was Maria's hand, rough-hewn and stiff from
extended hours of writing, nails nibbled to the quick. Her eyes
were moist, red, and she was lightly biting her lower lip with
tiny, perfect incisors. The four days in New York had rejuvenated her, but the last forty-eight spent cudgeling her brain,
combined with certain jet lag, had reinstated the unhealthy
pallor that seemed consonant with her impassioned composition. Her cheeks were slightly sunken. Her hair was disheveled
in an attractive sort of way, though dulled, and not at all supple.
She evinced the fatigue that I felt, and a scrutinizing third party
would probably not have been able to discern which of us had
been bedridden with influenza and which deskbound with genius. Such is the blurred demarcation between these two
domineering states.

She stretched out next to me, filling the slender space
between my sweat-drenched body and the edge of the bed. I
lifted my head from the pillow.

"Is it finished?" I asked.

"We must concentrate on making you well, mon ami," was
her manner of affirmative answer.

I relaxed, looked at the ceiling, began reassessing my
condition. Upon awakening in sickness, one recalls each area
of ache and detail of discomfort, hoping to see what the panacea
of sleep has accomplished. I noted that my fever had abated; the

hot and troublesome agitation was gone and the cavilling throb in my joints was the result of immobility rather than infection. My stomach gurgled. The realization of recuperation filled me with satisfaction and a generous goodwill.

"I've been disinclined to say this," I said, looking at the whorls of plaster on the ceiling, their array of twinkling mica dots that held bits of the room's light, "for fear of stating the obvious. We do not need to keep patting each other on the back and reinforcing the positive to establish . . . to recognize the value . . . the worth of something." Too long, I thought, you are prattling on too long.

"You are astounding," I said, "and I am hard-pressed to describe the magnitude of your work, the depth and breadth of your gift, and the gift you have given the world. Your book is a work of incredible virtuosity."

"*Tant pis,*" she murmured. I looked at her. Her eyes were closed and her lids blotchy. The sepia tar of tobacco tinged the cracks between her front teeth. There was a tiny, pinhead size pimple on her chin. The corners of her eyes showed the runnelled beginnings of wrinkles. Her hands, as I noted before, were ruddy, and mapped with a raised tangle of chalcedonic veins. The humbling effects of nature. Even as we achieve our loftiest intellectual heights, we must still contend with bugbites and boils, with the appearance of acne; we must rush off to relieve ourselves in the midst of world-rocking work; we get side-tracked in mid-equation by the damnable cramp of a menstrual cycle. A migraine can mangle a masterpiece. The brain is fascist; the body, egalitarian. The heavens do not give way; we are not granted immunity from disease. The magnificent products of the mind exist only for the intermittent joy and edification of others; to their creators they are Turkish delights left in the sun. Sickness and death are the great equalizers.

Thereafter, my recovery was swift, though my stomach was still a trifle delicate, my digestive system still not quite up to snuff, and anything more substantial than light broth, black currant tea, or a bit of filtered apple juice was impossible to keep down for the next few days. Though I still sported an unacceptable embonpoint, nearly two inches had melted from my outrageous waistline. My meager diet and the tumultuous churnings of my digestive track left me weak, and I tired easily.

My brain functioned as though I was well, though I did not immediately regain the strength that had seeped out of me.

But my redux—a *tromp l'oeil* shadow puppet which mimed a very convincing ratiocination—after so many grievous and gloomy days, bolstered my spirits. I suffered from the illusion of calm. The only irritation I experienced in my period of temporary contentment was an acute embarrassment over my recent, excessive behavior. What if my escapade at Mme Nerval's had resulted in my death. Or worse, discovery, arrest, incarceration. For too long now, I thought, my peevishness and pettifogging waylayed my attention to the mysteries and delights that were uppermost in my pantheon of pursuits. The most harmless creak, the most distant siren, the tiniest twinge in one's breast can balloon with angst and indecision if one lets it. Let the world take care of itself. Our labors had borne fruit (or vegetables, I dare say), the book was complete and, most important, Maria was still here. She had returned from New York and had slipped back into her work, back into her routine, as easily as one warms to a missed, genteel, soothing environment, as naturally as one climbs in next to the familiar, dreaming bedfellow who is so essential to one's passage into peaceful sleep. (If I gave any credence to hindsight, which I don't, I might be tempted to observe that my derisive fever was still raging, and the aforementioned euphoria was the froth of my boiling blood.)

Propped up in my bed, my pillows fluffed, a red bandeau loose around my throat, protected from chills by a roomy cotton bathrobe the color of unripened grapes and worn only on occasions such as this (something about a bathrobe, no matter how smart, always reminded me of illness: the pockets stuffed with moist, crumpled tissues, the lapels rife with the brisk smell of mentholated rub), I began rereading the dormant cantos of my epic poem. The pulse of rhythms, the ricochet of words, the hyperbole of image and idea were a surprise to me. Could I have possibly written all this? The remoteness of the voice that set these words to paper was startling enough, but the volume, the timbre, the *quantity*. There was prolificacy, there on the page, with blue annotations in my hand, with my characteristic typographical mistakes (I have a habit of typing "sould" for "soul" and "beguinning" when I should be "beginning"); there was proof, sheet after sheet of smeary, metrical, scribble-busy proof. What had ever made me think that such things were beyond my capacity? I read on with renewed interest, with gusto, and I even had the wherewithal to adjust a few adjectives, invigorate a few verbs.

And as I reclined there in my ill-fated splendor, Maria typed out a proof of her own introduction. I had offered to do it for her from dictation; I didn't think, I told her, that typing several pages would be so wearisome. But she insisted on doing it herself, claiming that she had watched me long enough and did not think typing was beyond her capabilities. It was a slow and spastic process, replete with expletives and puffing sighs of exasperation. She pecked out participles, scoured the clumsy and arcane keyboard for the corresponding marks that blended so easily, lyrically, and instinctively in her brain. But she slogged through it and, after tsking briefly over it, handed it to me for amendment.

For all the whiting out and angry strikeovers she indulged in, the typescript was remarkably clean. There were a few transpositions and an occasional misspelling. With my blue pencil—long warmed up and ready to run—I affixed casual suggestions, various clarifications, several thick question marks where I thought her musings could be better stated, a gaggle of exclamation points, one "lovely," one "very nice," and an all-cap "BRAVO" at the end. The only thing I feared, in returning it to her, was her finding my appended accolades gratuitous.

She came from the kitchen, where she'd fixed us tea in tiny porcelain cups with painted chinoiserie, and sat back at the desk with the corrected pages. Blowing on her tea, a shadow came over her face, a gauntness invaded her features, a spiral hank of black hair slipped free from behind her ear and lay in dark contrast against her cheek. Her lips were pursed, she shut her eyes briefly, and in the slight twitches and tics that enlivened her features I saw the look of one who is trying to swallow her temper. She rolled a clean sheet of paper around the platen of the Underwood and began grappling defiantly with the type-writer again. That the piece would retain its shape, syntax and tenor was, to me, ashamedly apparent. (There were stylistic modifications in the final published version, reflections that were reassessed in the skewed, tilting cheval glass of her mind and, tellingly, these were of ideas and images that I had singled out for praise. Though I do not think that there was any calculated maliciousness involved. But when I recognized them—Maria *disparue*, the thick, lavish book already a minor phenomenon and, in its refined, tidy, impressive hardcover form distressingly foreign to me, aloof and somehow not as contiguous with my life as its cruder prototype had been—they were the most piercing and heartrending notes in an already bittersweet pavane.)

I left my bed, and the preface left for New York the very next day. Its bon voyage was neither joyous nor celebratory. Labors of love are the temporary be-all but not the ultimate end-all. New loves and stranger loves follow; old labors reawaken; doubt and indecision glow in the darkness of our closed, tired eyes. Art is an oasis and Life is a parched, merciless continuum.

She dawdled and vacillated over details of the book's production. In her distracted reading, her actions about the apartment, her helter-skelter expeditions into the kitchen, I saw a recurrent restlessness, a lachrymose preoccupation, and something not unlike fear. Fear of the future and its undefinable shape: she was gazing into a kaleidoscope of whirling, colorful crystals, each design symmetrical and splendid, but each shifting with the slightest turn, never maintaining a preferred pattern. Everything fired her imagination but nothing quite fueled it. And details of her immediate environment, hitherto unobserved and insignificant, were suddenly points of consternation and contention: the fustiness of the atmosphere; the discoloration of the old paint on the walls; the refrigerator light, burned out now for some time; the dust and ashes that had settled in the most inaccessible crevices of the typewriter; the distracting cacophony of street sounds.

It fell upon her to supply a suitable book jacket photograph. If any aspect of *Spinacea oleracea* was fraught with indecision or lack of direction, it was this. She knew what she did not want: the photo should not bear any trace of the book's nature. Therefore, no kitchen shots, no Maria-in-her-apron, no food or cooking implements of any kind would be involved. And nothing that smacked of anything literary: no pencils or papers, no typewriter or desk of books, no "smug scholarship" or "intellectual conceit." I suggested a simple head shot, askance, eyes downward, a contemplative pietà, or a full frontal photograph of Maria's lovely, gentle features, or a sharp profile. (Or both—she raised her eyebrows, edged the tip of her tongue from the corner of her mouth, looked toward the ceiling, and briefly toyed with the idea of two photographs, side by side, in police blotter style—but finally vetoed it as glib, pretentious, and so lacking in convention that it would distract the reader from the book itself and encourage a brand of scrutiny and speculation inconsistent with her intentions. Certain critics may argue, good-naturedly, that though food is the pivotal character, it is the authoress' agile brain that is on display here. If this point has validity—and I believe it does—then what exactly were her intentions?)

But these, she said, lacked spontaneity, imagination and whimsical invention. For all the hours of close work, careful phrasing, painful restructuring and manic attention to linguistic detail, Maria still felt the book to be spontaneous and whimsical. I am in no position to dispute her. Such is the nature of the written word.

To explode connotations, to avoid a forced artfulness, what then? She wanted a setting that was a non-setting, a background that was a non-background. Her photograph should be, (to quote her contradiction) "of an area into which I can easily assimilate, and be easily assimilated, a hiding place in which I am clearly seen."

Without any concrete notions, she secured the services of a photographer for a Saturday afternoon. After careful consideration of the Yellow Pages, she settled on a fellow who specialized in "weddings—baby and pet portraiture," and who could only be reached by telephone "After six P.M." It was Maria's hope that a spare-time photographer, whose "professional" scope was limited to such narrow subject matter, would bring with him a simplicity of vision, a rigidity of style and content, and a lack of preconceived notions. Maria understood that the fellow might view the situation, upon arriving and getting started, as an opportunity to cut his aesthetic teeth, and cast his standard procedures to the winds of the avant-garde. But, she said, creative license on one's own time was one thing; creative license with a paying customer was something else, and she felt certain that she could guide the session. She believed that their combined naïveté and guarded experimentation might yield something innocent, something evocative, something that might capture the impalpable "feeling" she wanted the photo to possess, that their amatuerishness was their greatest asset in stumbling toward the surprise and charm of mutual discovery.

The fellow was young, only a year or two older than Maria and very plainly featured, not unattractive and yet not quite handsome. His shaven cheeks fairly glistened, like clean satin, and were exceedingly pale, from spending long hours in some darkroom perhaps, making innumerable poodle prints. The only facial feature not quite ordinary about him was a severe overbite which trivialized his serious, methodical manner as he fiddled and fumbled with tripods and light parasols. Much to Maria's contained delight—I could see she was making, at least initially, an effort to keep from smiling over much—he called her "Ma'am" and, after listening intently, politely deferred to her every suggestion. A second camera, a Polaroid black-and-white Instamatic, was set up on another tripod, and after her position and lighting had been fixed, he used it for the preliminary shot so that they could get a general approximation of positioning and composition. These "rushes," as he called them, gave Maria obvious pleasure. I would not have given them the slightest chance of hitting it off so well.

Maria herself was no less surprising. She was barefoot, in a pair of faded jeans with a deep blue patch on the left knee, and her sleeveless flannel shirt, knotted at the midriff, showing just the tiniest bit of her belly and the puckered top hemisphere of her navel. Her hair was unpinned, tumbling down over bare shoulders that were pearly in the klieg light. Excited and chatty, she laughed between shots, laughed at the draft photos, laughed at how serious she looked, "like some castrating *auteur*, some precocious film-festival sensation." The first shots were full-frontals of Maria standing against a stark off-white wall, her feet together, her hands behind her back. As there were no variations on this that she could quite see herself doing—he suggested she cross her legs, look away, look down, up, profile, three-quarters, crossed arms in front, hands in the pockets, but she just curled her lip and shook them all off—this was finished very quickly, and for several moments the three of us looked back and forth among each other, waiting for someone to suggest something else.

"Sitting down?" the photographer suggested. "In an open doorway?"

"Sitting down in an open doorway?" Maria laughed and bit her lower lip, looked down, shook her head, closed her eyes, and kept shaking her head as she was in the habit of doing when in deep thought. Finally she looked up with a smile and said, "The bathroom."

The space and illumination in our bathroom were equally meager, and there was not enough room to fit artist, subject and lamps. For the first time the photographer balked, saying he did not think it would be a very good idea, but Maria insisted. "Just use the light you have, no tripod, just shoot away," and that is what they did, sidling and squirming around one another, getting pictures of Maria leaning against a sink, sitting on the edge of the tub, sitting on the closed toilet, her legs crossed, her arms crossed, leaning against the doorframe, with her back to the medicine cabinet (a shot he protested vehemently against, claiming there was absolutely no room for angling, and that he couldn't execute the shot without getting a portion of himself in the picture, which was precisely what Maria wanted).

After exhausting all the positions and possibilities of our toilet facilities, Maria told him to pack up his things and bring them along to the wharf.

The sun was brilliant and hot. The bay and sky were comparable shades of blue, and could have melted deceptively into one another were it not for the relief of picturesque land masses—Alcatraz, the Tiburon shore—and the pleasure boats speckling the horizon like daubs of white from an artist's brush. The summer, with its long weeks of fine, temperate, unchanging weather, had arrived. The full complement of tourists had returned. These days, which had always recalled to me the normal reawakening of activity, the recapitulation of a soothing cycle, and had fueled me, in my simpler, solitary poet's time, with a feeling of metamorphosis, release, and vigor, now meant something else entirely. Bliss had gone bad, enlightenment was torn asunder. In the small puffs of clouds, tossed across the sky like a handful of stephanotis petals, I saw the image of the early Maria, the enchanting enigma, the phantom

shape that comprised my heart's desire. This image no longer
quickened my blood nor infused my head with strings of well-
linked words, but fixed in my field of vision a dwindling,
translucent, quixotic, mercurial memory, the afterglow of a
possibility, and I wished I had stayed home, indoors, leaving
Maria and the photographer to their own devices. Work on the
wharf and other matters would bring me face to face with the
dour countenance of these days soon enough. As he photographed her staring into the camera, standing at the rail of an
unused pier, I saw the Maria who watched me from a crowd as
I toiled at my job. As she posed on the balcony of a particular
bar, I saw the Maria who waited for me to arrive, contemplative
and distracted, in fiery sun spectacles. As he photographed her
in the Cannery, against a background of tourists and jugglers
and face-painting clowns, I saw the Maria of a certain languid
walk, quiet and self-assured, whose bemused interest in *me* was
the only known item of her innocent, alluring, mysterious
character. And after a couple of poses with a streetside harlequin
she accepted from him a pillow-shaped foil helium balloon,
which she took home and kept for several days, tied to the back
of the desk chair, before finally giving it to the boy down the
hall who tethered it to the handle of one of his many purloined
grocery carts.

For Maria, the photography session was a pleasing lacunae
in an otherwise grim plane. The rigors of writing had blurred
the days preceding it, and the rigors of stasis had stunted those
that followed. She appeared to be waiting, and yet there was
nothing for which to wait. Her involvement in the production
of *Spinacea oleracea* was, at most, a series of recommendations
and outright decisions. Hardly enough to reverse the atrophy
of creative paralysis. What she needed was something new, far-
reaching, forward thinking, consuming and intriguing, something to whet her artistic appetite. I believe she was slightly
overwhelmed by the massive, imposing void left by a completed
project, the sudden unexpected vacuum in which she flailed and
gasped, the seemingly untraversable abyss of the blank page,
the empty frying pan, the mocking, malignant grin of the
Cheshire future. She tinkered with the text, sent the adjusted
pages east, telling herself that certainly something could be
improved somewhere, some point could be embellished, some

element had been altered *sub rosa*, some subterfuge concerning her book was taking place.

She paced and pouted, was skittish about cooking, about diversions I suggested—shopping, a poetry reading, a jazz club— expressing enthusiasm and then falling into a funk once we'd undertaken these endeavors. I humbly asked her if she would peruse my epic poem, perpetually in progress, and she eagerly accepted. But the pages I pointed out to her stacked upon the desk sat unruffled, untouched. Her post-book sleeping habits were the inverse of those in her period of composition. To one who had observed her closely for so long, she appeared sloven and unkempt, not shaving her legs for days at a time. Upon awakening she sat listlessly on the edge of the bed, stared lackadaisically into the emptiness of the room, scratched her calves and yawned, or sucked her teeth, or chain-smoked over *The Gastronomic Hejira*, snorting and scribbling, slapping the notebooks shut in impatience. I refrained from asking about my poem, saving her the embarrassment of admitting she hadn't touched it, or saving myself the sting of her lie that she had and what she'd read was fine.

In the midst of all this was I, equally inept and unproductive, but attempting, however ridiculously, to reacquaint myself with my silent, leviathan work and be fruitful in the face of obvious decay. Hours of work saw the production of a single, slender line. Hours of rework left it but half a line, and careful, honest, objective re-evaluation left me with nothing at all. I would have preferred delusions or false feelings of grandeur. But cruel, bald-faced, lucid experience revealed, sans any redeeming quality or "A" for effort, that I was churning out crambo.

The air was fusty. Our eyes were dull and glazed with the patina of inertia. The more inactive she became, the more I wrote to no worthy end, lost in the voiceless muddle of headlong desperation. When she had been at her best I was blissfully, esoterically silent. Now, at her worst, I was a mess of raucous, senseless clamor.

Her compulsive piddling with the manuscript—addendum dashed off and sent to New York, brainstormy, probably incoherent letters of ideas, redundant instructions and extraneous cautions—were part of a self-fulfilling prophecy. If her editors gave such correspondence any serious consideration then confusion and misunderstanding could not be far behind. Maria's doting, confounding fears were shortly realized, as were mine.

A letter arrived. (We had no telephone. I hadn't a need for it though I suggested that we install one to facilitate coast-to-coast communication. But Maria said she preferred handling business by mail, since no one could instantly challenge her directives, or talk her into changing her mind over some detail or other. She also thought her prose was much more urgent and authoritative than her phone manner). The missive expressed confusion over some recent correspondence from Maria in which she, from what I could gather, specified the manner of each recipe's appearance in the text. From her scattered remarks and mumblings, and from the way she instructed me to prepare the typescript, recipes were to be integrated into the narrative flow and not necessarily separate and distinct. A given recipe might be referred to on page 72 and (floating self-consciously in smaller type), imprisoned in some box on page 74, causing backward and forward leafing and disrupting the linear progression. It appears, as you will note in your copy of *Spinacea oleracea*, that certain logistics of printing made this desire for strict linearity unrealistic in many instances, and separations occurred from time to time, despite her protests and probable cries of philistine sabotage. But far worse than this, much to Maria's red-faced, artery-bulging rage, was a recommendation that she consider a change of title. The demographics revealed that her book's potential buyers might very well balk at a product with a Latin name ("that, truthfully, rings of something botanical, scientific and text-bookish") and, though *her* decision was of course final, they would greatly appreciate it if she would look through the enclosed list of proposed alternatives, or send several of her own.

If not for her youthful vigor and health, Maria might very well have suffered a stroke or perished from an apoplectic fit upon reading such an unconscionable request. The letter was destroyed without much deliberation, only to be reconstructed so that, in her reply, she could quote verbatim this sentence or that, whatever evoked her most venomous disdain (though it would have been a better trick to find one sentence, other than

the dateline, that *didn't* evoke her most venomous disdain).
The "proposed alternatives" went something like this:

- Spinach
- The Spinach Patch
- The Spinach Garden: A Compendium of Green
  Delights
- A Little Green
- Viva la Verde: A Cornucopia of Spinach Delicacies
- A Vegetable Matter
- Spinach Revisited (prompting Maria to ask who had
  visited first)
- The Florentine Papers
- Emerald Cities ("This may or may not require you to
  change the title of Ch. 2")

There was nothing listless or dispirited in her response.
That she could reign her wrath long enough to sit and compose
a letter was a remarkable and impressive feat. She filled four or
so legal-size pages front and back with a cramped, incisive
hand. It was a letter dense with audacious renunciations,
scathing declamations, ripe asides—mostly concerning the suspect competencies of certain individuals—bitter barbs and
merciless, belittling ripostes. She was beside herself, and
utterly beyond me. When she had finished, she swept clean the
desktop with her trembling, frail white arms, sending airborne
pads and pencils, some books, various papers, a brimming
ashtray, a gooseneck lamp, a chipped porcelain teacup, and a
dictionary with a cracked spine. Then she put her face in her
hands and wept.

That night, her photographer arrived with several contact
sheets from their day-long session. She thanked him, paid him
for services rendered and promised to call him in a few days.
We checked the proofs closely, circling the ones we preferred
with an orange grease pencil. She sat at the desk. I pulled the
coffee table up behind her and looked on, pointing out my
favorites. My low seat put me level with her bare shoulder. It
was decorated with tiny cocoa freckles and, at its peak, a
blanched dime-sized vaccination scar that evoked for me an
onslaught of eidetic images both real and unreal: Maria on the

sun-bathed balcony; Maria on the streetcorner clutching her notebooks; Maria behind me on some rostrum; Maria with dirty knees sinking tulip bulbs into some rich soil. As these slowed and faded and I returned to my time and place and position, I leaned over and kissed that raised, smooth scar. Maria turned to me, smiled—a weak smile, rueful, piteous and stained with a meaning that delineated all the tangles and sinuous intertwinings and twisting sins she possessed, that were beyond my capacity to unravel—then took a pair of pinking shears from the drawer and cut the proofs in zig-zagged pieces.

She would go to New York in two days.

"They are going to bury me, mon ami, if I am not there to shake off the dirt."

"I know."

"You understand. I'm helpless here. Dead in the water. Stuck on a sandbar."

I looked toward the desk, repopulated now, books, blank pages and pencils in orderly, impossible piles.

"Floundering . . ." she said.

"I understand. You needn't explain."

"The hejira must go on. You've seen what it's been like here. I . . . neither of us can . . ."

I turned away, closing off her words, and watched a fly slowly scale the wall and disappear between the crack of the doors that concealed the Murphy bed.

"I said I understand. You're not coming back this time."

"Now, who can say? When all this business is finished . . ."

"You won't be coming back."

She was not embarrassed or contrite, not defensive or confrontational or even matter-of-fact, but simply, unquestionably, Maria.

"I can't lie to you as I did poor Violet. You know me too well, mon ami."

And with that untruth, she left me.

POSTSCRIPTUM

S omehow, I was found. An attentive, rapacious eye, perhaps, gazing where it was not permitted, found Maria's San Francisco address and passed the information along. Or perhaps it was a slip by agent or editor. Who knows? Whatever the circumstances, I was approached enough times that I've lost track, with questions and offers and pleas for any bit of information of a personal or professional nature, for any photograph or insight into the inscrutable authoress of *Spinacea oleracea*. For the first time in my entire career of literary pursuits, I *received* uninitiated correspondence from agents. But they were not interested in my poetry. I was even personally approached at work on the wharf one afternoon—breezy, wads of cloudlets skimming toward the Golden Gate—by a gentleman who wondered if I would be interested in reviewing the book for a certain Bay Area publication. Hissing some choice language under my breath—so as not to be heard by the young boy I was waiting on—I declined.

This did not all happen immediately. Maria's publishers were generous enough in their promotional budget, and the first reviews elicited a flurry of interest. But the ad sizes slowly dwindled, some crotchety stiff-necked reviews appeared, and the book's sales seemed to flag slightly. Though I do not have any documented proof of this, I assumed as much, because I received a letter from one of Maria's people at the publishing house suggesting for her own good and good of a fine book, that I write her and try to persuade her to go public and begin promoting her own work. I did not respond.

Their worries were soon alleviated by a queer canard that appeared in an Eastern paper. It was suggested by some smug agitator that *Spinacea oleracea* was published pseudonymously by a certain, long-standing, influential epicure. Such an irresponsible bit of speculation created a minor brouhaha; denials were made, disclaimers claimed, retractions demanded. But such a minor occurrence caught the attention and sparked the curiosity of a small audience, who passed their interest on to others. Even the most ridiculous musings, not grounded in any kind of reality, wholly intended to cause scandal and sensation, to some degree become plausible once they find their way into print. How much the book itself, however, assisted in prodding the public's imagination is incomputable.

Then a brief item appeared, picked up by the local paper, of a minor incident that pushed the book and Maria past the point of bemused interest and into the bubbling pot of faddishness. It seems that a woman wandered into Brentano's one afternoon and began autographing copies of *Spinacea oleracea*, much to the delight of browsing patrons, until the manager broke up the excitement, exposed the fraud, and sent the hoaxer packing. But the event, apparently insignificant and modestly reported, served to mythicize Maria even more. Wrote one columnist, picking up on the story: "but no one, it seems, can say just what she looks like. Passionate about her anonymity, her publisher protects her, and that bookstore manager might very well have unwittingly ejected the invisible author. What a story he'll have to tell his grandchildren as they leaf through their copy of this immense, maddening, scintillating book . . ."

I had no interest in cashing in on a craze, in betraying and bankrupting the rich, brief time I had in Maria's company, though I felt abysmal, wretched, bitter, cheated out of my former occupation and preoccupations by an amalgam of my own sloth and selflessness. I felt as if my powers had been drained from me. I was followed by a slouching, soundless, self-pitying silhouette.

She was certainly gone, and yet . . . the floodgate did not open, the old life did not return; I could not even harness my melancholy and produce something that even vaguely resembled the voice of the poet I once was. Was he simply dead inside me, or had he gone with her? And where had she gone? Where did she come from? Is she my problem, or is she the key to my problem?

I began making discreet inquiries based on the bits and pieces of information offered by her over the course of the relationship. Many things were misleading, dead ends, or lies that did not fit into the developing picture. But information—history, the past—once it exists, always exists, like unidentified microbes floating through the air of our rooms, and one needs only persistence, patience, and a jigsaw sense of rearrangement to draw it out and slip the strange shapes together. One need only find the link, the key to the code, the incidental easily passed over scrap that makes things intelligible, that serves as legend to the arcane map of the past.

I was very fortunate in this regard. This chronicle would not have been written otherwise, though at the time I was only gathering information for information's sake. In my free hours I explored the Tenderloin, not expecting to find anyone or anything that would necessarily be revelatory but to get a sense of the place, the impoverished, dire urgency of existence, the squalor of bohemia, and, in my wanderings, a clue of where to begin. I had hoped some idea, some blandishment would cross my path. But the Tenderloin, more than anything, gave me a feeling of greater remoteness. There was nothing artistic in its decay, nothing inspirational or ennobling in its poverty. My desire for knowledge was blanketed at the end of most days by despair and revulsion.

Finally, I left the Tenderloin to act out its own stark, derisive fantasy unobserved by me. Traces of Maria had effectively vanished.

Stymied and weary, I returned to my old routine—though I did not resume my visits to Mme Nerval's House—but these activities were hollow, mechanical. They had no particular purpose behind them and absolutely no zest. I returned to my desk for evenings of silence, perused bookstores where the rows of spines had incomprehensible titles, sat in taverns that served drinks without flavor and had patrons without voices. I knew I must do something to break my mental degradation, that my brain, my movements, my habits, my emotions, were collapsing incrementally, and that I was approaching a state of entropy, but this very collapse and decay made it impossible for me to come to terms with just what it was I had to do.

One Saturday afternoon as I dawdled about a bookshop, the change began. There was nothing remarkable about the place. I had been there several times over the years hoping to discover something surprising and rare in its inventory, but usually came away disappointed. This day, at first, did not seem any different. The radio behind the counter played something baroque. The proprietor, a middle-aged man with a large bald spot and horn-rimmed glasses, was leaning over a back issue of *Playboy*, casually and evenly turning the pages, as if each soft and oily body were just another advertisement. And there, surrounded by the musty smell of aging pages, the weak light absorbed by so many dark covered books, was the haunting feeling of a presence, a creeping, insinuating swirl of recognition, the slow, taunting assimilation of some sensory data culled and stored, but not immediately understood. I retraced my steps gingerly, anxious, expectant, unsure of what was about to happen, when my eyes fell upon, for perhaps the hundred-and-first time, a painting hanging on the wall behind the counter. A tingling sensation told me something lurked, a tinnitus that squelched the radio buzzed through my left ear, and I scoured the picture—a gouache, soft pastel aquas and beiges and birch grays of a pier, boats, water, a grassy knoll jutting up in the background—until finally I caught my breath as I discerned, in the lower right-hand corner, a flourished and confident "Cubby." Events shaped themselves, futures expanded, agents of entelechy ballooned to monstrous sizes; radiant atoms, incensed and excited, rushed into small pockets of my brain and released a quantum measure of energy so intense, an Absolute Moment so dense with understanding and realization that I thought I would implode, and the powerful gravity I exuded would cause the books, the shelves, the shop owner to pull loose and accelerate toward me, becoming pure energy trapped forever in the black pocket of the instance.

"Where did you get that?" I said, transfixed, staring at the work. Perhaps he looked at me, at the painting. I can't say. Perhaps he just knew, in the magic of the strange event, what I was talking about.

"I bought it," he said. The sound of pages turning.

"When? From whom?"

I looked at him finally, and he was studying me over the rim of his spectacles, still turning the pages as if he were looking at them.

"From some woman. A long time ago."

The colors swam and had the brilliance and luster of daylight, of vigor.

"The artist?"

"Yeah. Twenty years ago or so. You like it?" he said.

"Yes. I like it."

"Whattaya think it's worth?" he pushed the magazine aside, folded his arms across the counter.

"Whatever you say it's worth."

He yawned, looked over his shoulder at the painting, scratched his cheek, looked back at me.

"I say it's worth twenty thousand bucks. You give me twenty thousand bucks and I'll give you that picture, the store, the books, and all the other paintings just like it I got piled up in the back."

"You have more? The same artist?"

"Yeah. Lots. I used to . . . know her, ya' know. A long time ago."

In his storage room, amidst empty cartons and bundles of periodicals, canvasses were stacked against a wall beneath a dusty, water-stained sheet. Other artists were interspersed throughout, but most of the paintings were Cubby's. Like the one out front, they were simple, colorful landscapes with bold, thick brushstrokes. There were some drip paintings that I recalled Maria mentioning on one occasion, and some grim, inept chiaroscuros that were a complete surprise. Most of the canvasses had suffered some degree of water damage. Colors bled. Oils cracked. One aquarelle had a rip.

"I bought a lot of her stuff. Five bucks apiece. When she quit painting and sold everything. She had a kid. Art wasn't important to her anymore. But I bought 'em up, ya' know. Maybe I liked 'em or something. Maybe I thought they'd be worth something someday. That's how Gertrude Stein got the ball rolling."

"Yes," I said, half-listening, holding up and examining a Cubby Pengguling original of a park with benches and eucalyptus trees. "How much, really?"

"I told you. Twenty K."

"Do I look like I have twenty thousand dollars?"

"I don't know what you look like, Ace," he sneered and walked out into his store.

I looked at each painting for several moments. I even examined the ones not painted by Cubby, hoping to translate their scrawl of a signature, to glean the name of someone who might have known her from that time. But I could not make them out.

Out front, the bespectacled proprietor was looking at another magazine until I approached. He stared at me conspicuously.

"I know her daughter," was all I said. "The kid you mentioned. I just thought she might be interested in seeing these." He reached under the counter and clicked off the radio.

"Look, I don't care. You can have the whole bunch of them for a hundred bucks. Really. Serious price. No haggling."

"I'll have to go get the money."

I did not have a hundred dollars, but my employer—generally an uncompromising man, but not one who is blind to dedication and dependability—gruffly gave me the advance. And our bookshop owner, at the sight of the cash, was far less cryptic and reticent on my second visit, and explained to me how he had known her, his brief involvement with the communal coterie, and the names of some of the people he remembered from that time. He warned me that many might very well be dead—such was the extremity of their habits—or, even worse, respectable, and therefore unwilling to talk to me. I mentioned Mrs. al-Habim, Maria's early ersatz mother, the only name I knew from that time besides Cubby's, and the proprietor matter-of-factly informed me that he had forgotten completely about her until just a year ago, when he read of the old woman's death in a nasty mugging incident. And I am sorry, Maria, that you had to find out this way.

I looked up addresses, made inquiries by mail, by pay phone, by personal encounter. These were not always fruitful, but it was not so much the necessity of piecing together an enigmatic past as it was the activity of investigation itself that was therapeutic. It lifted me from my gloomy struggles. For a few splendid, distracting moments, my sorrows were secondary. The well would certainly run dry, perhaps soon, and all the information I had the physical means to gather would be gathered, but that was a bridge I was careful not to cross prematurely. I did not want to consider the consequences. And in the back of my mind all my fingers were crossed that circumstances would somehow take care of themselves.

Maria's twenty-fourth birthday discreetly arrived, the day after Shakespeare's 420th, and my heart was plagued with pangs of longing and wistful, sentimental tenderness. By that time I had learned the cacophonous nature of her birth, her odd upbringing and the flickering episodes of her early prodigiousness. The day—April 24: maddening, coincidental, mysterious and meaningful April—was thick and ponderous with significance now. My every move was cautious. I checked the sky for omens, was particularly careful crossing streets, made a determined effort to identify and avoid suspicious characters around the wharf. The teeming crowds crawled by, the touring bikes juked and jounced and rung their bells. I was fretful, addled, looking involuntarily over my shoulder. I committed errors in making change. As the morning progressed, as the sun slid across the sky, so did an arduous desire for Maria's physical presence grow within me. My agitation was apparent and crippling. My employer asked me what the problem was. I feigned illness, something I had never done before, and begged to be allowed to go home. It suddenly became imperative that I go there where Cubby Pengguling's paintings—now up, adorning my walls in a vain, uninspired attempt to recreate Maria's childhood environment—beckoned me to examine them for the umpteenth time. The safe and copacetic colors of Maria's natal world, on that day, seemed to be the habitat I required. And hurrying there, I passed a sidewalk espresso bar and was overcome with the disquieting feeling that someone's eyes were tracking me. As I looked toward the crowded tables, the mass of customers, the scuttling waiters, my gaze fell immediately upon Violet. I had virtually given up trying to find her. Her old—their old—apartment was long vacant with no forwarding address, and she maintained no phone listing. Our looks linked for but a fraction of a second, as she immediately reverted her stare back to her demitasse, but it was too late; her fierce, poisonous, seething glance had made its way to me through the disturbed, crackling, preoccupied air.

As I wove toward her through the maze of tables, she gathered up her newspaper, her shoulder bag, and attempted to flee. "Wait," I shouted, sidling between chairs, jarring the elbow of a man in a white poplin suit who was raising a cup of cappuccino to his lips. A comet's tail of coffee arced across the table, splashed across the shoulder of his shrieking female companion. People were ducking, chairs slid about and butted together and two of them pinned me at the thigh and held me fast. The man in the poplin suit rose and growled curses, the heavily waxed ends of his hideous handlebar mustache twitching like antennae; someone was blithering in Greek, or Italian; someone had my shirtfront; something tore. And Violet, lithe, maneuvering much more efficiently than a chunky, paranoid, poltroonish poet, slipped free, escaping down the street, never looking back.

In my room, disheveled and breathless, I slumped into my armchair, fixed my eyes on the painting across from me, on creases and fractures in the impasto, waiting for my anxiety to subside. But it would do nothing of the sort. It grew worse. What is it that throws one into this constant flux, that gives one fear, fits of despondency, of anger, of loathing? What is it that leaves one repulsed with himself and in constant dread of others? Why does the sight of a certain someone cause one to lose frail composure, to flee, to affect ignorance? I felt a certain kinship with Violet; we were partners in similar miseries. The damage we'd sustained was our commonality. We could not rescue one another from despair, or the source of that despair, but it is much easier to remain afloat when we see another in the distance treading water just as madly.

But Violet could not know my situation. Or could she? Perhaps that is what caused her haste and alarm, the sorrow in my eyes: the tainting of grief that pinched and pulled my features; the rending tone of my plaintive voice as I called to her. When we are unsightly we avoid mirrors. And perhaps in seeing me, Violet caught an unexpected, opprobrious reflection, sad and sobering.

And here was my hall of mirrors, I thought, crossing to the painting, fingering some cracked emerald, some striated cornflower blue. Reflections of defunct endeavors, a sudden dearth of wherewithal, the desuetude of creation. A gambit gone awry.

And as I touched the canvas—another pastoral scene, an immense park in spring, backed by a boskage of trees with brush-tipped blossoms of white and red and tiny picnickers on a pinkish blanket, too far away and small for features, just vaguely human shapes right of center, but in Cubby's coy and self-conscious way, the focal point of the picture—the figures began to shift and dance, just vibrating at first, but then jumping noticeably. I blinked hard, backed away, and saw the entire canvas shaking. A thunderous rumble swelled up through the floorboards, filling the room with a deep drone and shudder. The painting fell from its nail, as did another, and another, as if an invisible spirit were running through the room, flipping them off the wall one by one. An old jam jar filled with pencils pogoed across the desk and lept to a shattering death. Cupboard doors swung open and disgorged saucers and glasses. The medicine cabinet dropped a can of shaving cream into the basin with a loud thunk. The lights flickered, the windows rattled; the Murphy bed parted its doors and fell booming to the floor. Everything was movement, dance, clattering and clinking song. And by the time I realized it was an earthquake and dove beneath my desk, it was over.

I stayed there for some minutes, the experience finally frightening me in retrospect. The city had gone inordinately quiet: that silent moment of assimilation, as when someone pops a balloon in a crowded room, halting all conversation for several pregnant seconds. Then the hum and rush started again, vigorously. Briefly reminded of our fragile, precarious position here, we resumed life with a greater urgency. I finally emerged. Though momentary and relatively mild, it was undoubtedly a full-fledged quake and not a tremor. I threw open a window and looked out onto the street. No damage was readily apparent; no one felled by plummeting pieces of edifice. I carefully reassembled my apartment and tensed for aftershocks, but none would come for several hours. Horns sounded outside, busses roared. The street was busy again. Sirens screamed closer and closer, approaching my block, then screamed past my building. I leaned out the window again, looking up and down to ascertain if it were these apartments suddenly ablaze. Other tenants were doing the same, but we saw no smoke. The trucks kept on by. Straining to see what could be burning so near, I finally noticed a sweet smell to the air—vanilla, almond, and cherry scents—and then the rotten malodorous stench of cigar smoke, or something very much like cigar smoke, but far more powerful, as if a thousand cigars were burning at once. As I mulled this over briefly and considered what it could be, a cold, riveting terror raced through me. I clambered out onto the fire escape, ran down the ladder—an action that aroused my neighbors, who shouted questions at me as I passed, and, getting no answer, began to flee the building as well—and lept to the sidewalk, contorting my ankle. The hot pain that swarmed through my leg was brief, however, and could not hinder me as I did a kind of skip-run-limp toward the tobacconist's shop that housed Mme Nerval's.

The area was cordoned off. Police cars, ambulances, and fire trucks were angled in harum-scarum, their rotating emergency lights bounding off and sweeping across faces and facades; high pressure hoses directed long arms of water into shattered windows and onto the smouldering roof. A girl in a black lace peignoir jumped from a second-story ledge into an outstretched net, much to the delight of all the spectators, who cheered uproariously, less for her courage than for the revealing nature of her bare-bottomed flight. A man in a business suit, carrying jacket and tie, his shirt open, his hirsute stomach exposed, lept about on one foot trying to slip on a shoe and make a getaway through the crowd of onlookers. I shuffled through the crowd on the sidewalk, through the gaping pedestrians, police, and weeping, half-naked prostitutes, searching for Yvette. The air was rank with smoke and heat; the burning building was spitting and rumbling. I grabbed the arms of the women and spun them around to look into their faces, one after another, until I had finally found Mme Nerval herself. Her mouth was crabbed and pinched tight, her pince-nez sat cock-eyed on her nose. For a second or two I stared at her; a silence encased us amidst the frantic hubbub. "Yvette?" I said, and with an open palm she struck me across the face with a force far beyond that of a woman of such small stature. The fierce shot seared my cheek, my head swam, my eyes crossed. I reeled a bit and went down on one knee to the pavement. Tears welled up from the sting of the blow, but I grabbed her firmly planted ankle, looked up into her twisted, hideous features, still waiting for an answer. She simply shook free her foot and looked back toward the terrible conflagration.

Yvette's name appeared in the paper. She was described as a "tenant." Investigation determined that the blaze began in her room—the result of unattended candles, the jolt of the earthquake, the bed rapidly catching fire. The building was, as I noted some time ago, old, without modern fire prevention systems, and the flames and smoke spread too rapidly for any kind of containment.

This pitiful occurrence is in no way connected with the events depicted in this chronicle. I cannot assume or assign responsibility for her senseless death. I cannot. Though my conscience and my memory—two terrible things—egg me on.

But to accept this tragedy as a result of my sins would be too paralyzing, a psychic suicide, and would do nothing to amend what has happened. And I would cease to function. That I have found the mettle to undertake this memoir is itself a tiny miracle. Each day begins on tenterhooks.

The painful recreation of my relationship with Maria Perpetua and its attendant events has set off in me, like a string of firecrackers, image after stroboscopic image of her: tableaux and tender episodes that did not find their way into this chronicle. Absent is the time she literally dragged me by the shirt cuff throughout Chinatown, from *dim sum* to *dim sum*, sampling and recording the distinguishing characteristics of countless dumplings, many of which were incorporated in her very own spinach and pork version. When they'd been perfected, you set the steaming plate before me, leaned in close to drizzle your own sorrel-colored spiced oil over them, and—with your bent head wreathed in those marvelous vapors, a bit of bottom lip held between your teeth—your eyelids delicately fluttered, from a rare throb of genuine rapture: an instant of bliss that I never detected, despite my heartsick scrutiny, in our nonculinary intimacies. I have also inadvertently omitted your nearly disastrous mad dash up the stairs of our building with a tureen of green, viscid wedding soup (a loose carpet runner, a spectacular bit of balance to avoid scalding) for sampling by Mrs. Diagiacomo, our landlord's mustachioed wife, who reeked of Ben-Gay, remember, and much to your chagrin saved the marble-sized meatballs for last. Nor have I complained, as I did not complain then, about the day you commandeered the desktop—this very desktop, once wet with your frustrated tears— to stretch out your tortillas and spread them with cream cheese, shredded spinach, fresh basil, and sunflower seeds, roll them, and slice off finger sandwiches that have now found fame as "Tiburon Pinwheels." There are many other moments I cannot recount here, not due to modesty or tact, but because they are too frail, too subtle, to be properly appreciated. I could not bear so many disinterested fingerprints on my most cherished possessions.

But, more than memories and their magic details, I have found something else, something more personally edifying, for only in writing of Maria have I felt the stirrings and glimmers that were once so familiar to me. Only by undertaking this fresco have I approached the sedate verbal realm in which I once resided. And though I took up my pen only as a last resort, as an emollient to a constantly chafing despair and creative dysfunction, I have experienced, from moment to moment of composition, the purling, swarming narcotic, the euphoria of language, the supple and pliable media of words. Without them, I realize how ungainly and unsatisfactory, how nearly unlivable my life will be.

But if I can only write of Maria, the fullness of her infamy, the underside of her fame, the juggernaut of her genius, what then? If I can only wax prosodically on one small episode in my life, one blinding magnesium period, on an Absolute Moment from which there is neither absolution nor escape, then so be it. This is the clever hell the gods have fashioned for me: the poet locked in his own prose prison. The only measure available to mitigate his pain, his only respite from sorrow, is his meticulous depiction of its source. And as the project wanes, the pain again borders on the unendurable, the world slopes into the inarticulate, and yet . . . well, let me just begin by saying that during the months of research and composition pursuant to the publication of Maria Perpetua's much-heralded *Spinacea oleracea*, it was *I*, take note, and I alone who was her tester, her taster, her collaborator. Her long-suffering lover. Her muse.